About the Author

Edward Vass grew up in Devon, before leaving to study at the University of Lincoln. After graduation, he left the UK to teach English in the South Korean city of Daegu. He now works in London, and lives just outside of Brighton with his family. *Milton in Purgatory* is his debut novella.

Milton in Purgatory

EDWARD VASS

Fairlight Books

First published by Fairlight Books 2019

Fairlight Books
Summertown Pavilion, 18-24 Middle Way, Oxford, OX2 7LG

A CIP catalogue record for this book is available from the
British Library

1 2 3 4 5 6 7 8 9 10

ISBN 978-1-912054-36-7

www.fairlightbooks.com

Printed and bound in Great Britain by Clays Ltd

Designed by Sara Wood

Illustrated by Sam Kalda
www.folioart.co.uk

For all the people that helped me become the man I am today, and have now passed on.

Preface

15 seconds before

...Inhale...
A snigger escapes my lips.
...Exhale...
My defence against situations I can't handle.
...Inhale...
The tarmac is cold.
...Exhale...
I think my leg is broken.
...In...
Burning in my chest.
...Out...
This is wrong.
...In...
I've never tasted blood before.
...Out...
It's sweet.
...In...
...Out...

Only twenty-six.
...In...
...Out...
I'll just close my eyes for a minute.

...

I

1 hour 34 minutes before

Everything is dark and everything is quiet.

You find me huddled in the early hours of a Monday morning. Deep enough in sleep that I still believe the dreaming world's fanciful imaginings, but awake enough to consider that they may make me late for work.

The clock ticks over to 7.30am. Music delves into my sleepy mind – a dawn chorus of 'Waterloo Sunset'. From these depths my dreamy ears fail to process such earthly sounds. Bewildered as I am, my journey to consciousness isn't helped by the Kinks' message of lazy afternoons and sunset paradises. Finally, the song finishes and sleep retreats like a meandering tide from the shore. I open my eyes.

I fumble for the snooze button on the radio – no more music. Goddamn, I have a hangover. Feels like a rhino is making love to my head, not tender love either, this is wild, angry love. I wipe the angel shit

9

from the corners of my eyes and flick it onto the floor. They're really crusty. Went to a local pub last night for a few beers with friends, and then a few more on my own. The rest of the evening and the trip home are a blur, but I got home so that's the main thing.

As I stretch my extremities to every corner of the bed, a strange squawk escapes my lips. That was unexpected. I don't have a girlfriend to wake with bizarre morning noises, so instead I roll over to check if I've woken my hamster. Nope, Penfold Fingerstick is still sound asleep in his little blue cage perched on my bedside table. 'Penfold!' I croak. 'Penfold, are you awake?' Nothing. Lazy bastard. 'Penfold, I have the worst hangover.' My voice crackles deep in my dried throat. I swallow. 'Why do you let me drink like this?' I rub my aching eyes. 'I'm never drinking again.'

I let out a long, almost otherworldly groan that feels like it could continue indefinitely. I'm not in complete control of any of my bodily functions. A piss might help. I can't be bothered going all the way downstairs to the bathroom. The sink in the corner of my bedroom will do. Rolling out of bed, I stumble in the general direction. Going to the toilet in my bedroom sink isn't the most glorious sight first thing in the morning, but as I said, I'm single, so who cares. I think I'm going to be sick. For dignity's sake I concentrate hard on holding it back. I do have a line.

Slumping back into bed, I make the most of the last few, lingering minutes of peace before I have to get up for work. I sprawl on my back and let my throbbing eyes drift round the room. The low ceiling and clammy air are suffocating. A single bulb hangs naked in the darkness. In the gloom I can't convince my eyes to focus on it; instead they travel to the peeling, green oval-pattern wallpaper to my left. The chaotic design stirs my stomach. My eyes drop to the lightly charred grey tile fireplace below. One of the tiles is chipped, I think, from a drunken game of indoor golf. Sentimental junk runs the length of its mantel: a typewriter teapot, couple of postcards, a cheap wall phone I haven't bothered to attach to the wall, a toy car collection that I hate and a varied selection of grooming products from past Christmases and birthdays. No idea why I keep this stuff but can't seem to let it go.

At the end of my bed the floor is covered by clothes. I call this my floor-drobe. Beyond that a chipboard desk sits in a large bay window. When the curtains are open the window looks out to a generally quiet slice of terraced world on a quiet street in Cowley, a little east of Oxford's stuffy core. It's a den of carefree magic cafés, nighthawk pubs and restaurants to suit any tongue. The dawning sun shoots pale beams from behind the curtains into this dusty gloom.

A sigh that sounds far more pained than I expect trickles from me as my head drops to the right. My television is on. Apparently, I checked the football scores on teletext last night. I scan the results – Spurs 2 Liverpool 1 – thank God, we needed that. An *X-Files* video is sticking out of the recorder's post-box slot. I normally watch an episode or two after a few drinks, but I don't remember doing it last night.

A massive wardrobe, way too big for the limited space, sits like an elephant that's unwittingly attended a picnic in a Wendy-House. This oversized mahogany monstrosity only just allows space for my bedroom door leading out to the corridor.

Rolling to the side of the bed, I let my head hang over the side. Is that sick in my bin? Holding my breath, I shuffle forward an inch or two. Oh dear God, it *is* sick – what an abomination. 'I'm never drinking again,' I reiterate to Penfold, who still hasn't risen.

I stare vacantly at a book beneath the bin. *Pictures of Cuba* lies open. Gingerly, I lift the bin. There's a halo of sick circling Ernest Hemingway's Havana home – fitting, I guess. When I was seven, an uncle of mine who'd been working out there gave it to me. He was only a vacuum salesman, but to me he was an adventurer. Hemingway's home is a revolutionist, alcoholic, bear-fighter's dream. A small, unassuming summer house with shelves of well-thumbed hardbacks overlooked by the mounted heads of Hemingway's hunting trophies. Paintings and sketches of remote climes scatter the walls; one of Hemingway with his white wispy beard in full safari suit, grasping a hunting rifle in one hand and resting the other on a dead leopard. And, of course, the drinks trolley sits like an obedient old dog next to his favourite chair.

Pictures of Cuba still gives me the same urge for adventure that it did on the very first time of reading. It reminds me of the sort of person I want to be. Even with this toxic stew behind my eyes, the same warm glow of limitless possibilities washes through my veins. The experiences I'd have if I got out of this place, the people I'd meet, the women I'd meet! Maybe I'll leave all this in two or three years; I'll see how the mortgage is looking.

There's a rustling at the end of the bed. 'Penfold? Is that you? You sneaky little bastard. How did you get out of your cage?' Upturning towards the sound, I'm dazzled by light from a gap in the curtains. This slice of the outside world is too much to bear. I squint as coloured bars bounce round my tired eyes, creating a shape, a female shape. A trick of the light, surely. I blink rapidly, close my eyes, breathe and try to clear my vision. I open my eyes. The figure remains.

Someone's there – cold reality shudders through me. I shoot bolt upright in bed and press my back to the headboard. 'What the fuck?' How is it possible? Who is she? Am I in danger? The ghostly figure just stands with her back to me, unmoving. Nervous breaths tremble in the moment. How can this be anything more than imagination? But my imagination isn't this good. I try to rub the deception from my eyes, but still she stands, silhouetted by the morning sunshine. Did I pull last night? How did I forget that? I breathe, and squint at the shadows of her form. No doubting it, she's there, standing with her back to me, at the end of my bed, naked. Where did she come from? How did I not see her? Was she lying on the floor? My eyes work their way up her body, fighting hard to remain on course until they break through the scattered rays of light bouncing hypnotically from a completely bald head.

I need to see her face, maybe it'll jog my memory. I unstick my dry lips. 'Hello?'

She says nothing. Just stares into the light.

I try again. 'Hello?'

Nothing. I edge forward to the end of the bed. My mouth opens to speak again, but I decide to stand and reach out my trembling fingers instead. Just half a metre separates us. Between two alluring dimples sits a delicate little shell-shaped birthmark. Just an inch away from her paper-white skin, I suddenly hear a sound. Music. Her head turns slightly. I gasp. 'You hear it.' She spins to face me. Her eyes are closed. Our noses almost touch. I can taste her breath. Smell her sweat. Her face is otherworldly, but before I can understand why, her eyes snap open. In them I see… Heaven. I stumble backwards into the path of the morning sun. Instinctively, my eyes snap shut as I tumble onto the bed. As quickly as my eyes close, they open. She's gone.

Was I dreaming? It seems lighter, like time has moved on. I glance at the clock. *7.45am.* Quarter of an hour has passed. Must have been a dream. It felt so real.

The unease from this daybreak rendezvous is enough to get me up. To be sure, I check the end of the bed, under the desk and behind the curtains – zilch.

I concentrate on keeping a steady pace along the landing outside my bedroom and down the curved wooden staircase. I squint through the haze. Holding both banisters, I lower myself to the cold hallway floor and shuffle to the bathroom. It's a tip. I'm way too tired to care. I stumble through the used shampoo bottles and old loo rolls scattered across the floor and flick the shower on. Leaning heavily on the bathroom sink, I sigh stale breath onto the shaving mirror and try to shake the strange feeling that hangs to me like yellow on teeth.

This face of mine – it's so bland. I've seen hundreds of people this week with faces so ordinary their images drained from my mind the moment my eyes left them. One of them could have been me. Standard-issue male, four-pound haircut and brown scruffy beard, patch up with the misgivings and desires of a high percentage of the populace and that's pretty much it. What the fuck am I on about?

There's a cut on my lip. Poking it with my tongue, I notice the inside of my mouth is swollen. I remember, vaguely, I got punched. Yeah, that's it, some alcoholic arsehole punched me off my bar stool. Don't remember why, but I do remember ramming my stool into his jaw and knocking him down with a messy right hook. The rest isn't too clear, but I think bouncers and the pavement were involved. Why does this shit always happen to me?

I boxed a bit when I was young so have always felt comfortable throwing a punch. Less so receiving one, but nine times out of ten it's just a graze rather than anything that leaves a mark. Dad signed me up at eleven when I got beaten up three times in my first week of secondary school. Wasn't too bad either – even fought for a local club for a while, until Mum shut my hand in the car door when I was fourteen. I lost my three middle fingers at the knuckle. Wish I could have kept it up. Even at the tender age of thirteen I noticed the extra attention boxing got me from the opposite sex. I miss it. Feels like the last time I achieved anything. It taught me to stand tall. I'm well known in my social circles for my high chin, wrenched-back shoulders and military-esque stance. People always tell me I make them feel like they should stand up straighter. I think it's a compliment, but it never sounds like one. The rest of my early good intentions have been lost to the mists of time, ready meals and adolescence.

Steam from the shower makes its way across the mirror and my brutalised mouth disappears. Probably best. I look at the selection of toothbrushes and pick the lesser of three evils. As I brush, the memory of my naked, bald dream woman blooms in the dark recesses of my hangover. What a clear dream. I can remember the moment perfectly; the exhilaration is seared into me. God, I need to find a real woman, not just an imaginary one. Having brushed for what feels like a sensible amount of time, I climb into the shower to wash my strange morning dreams away.

I'm mostly dry and part-dressed when back in my bedroom my hangover rears its unsteady head again. With one sock on and the other hanging from the end of my toe, I slump down on the side of the bed. I really can't be bothered with work today. I could pull a sicky. No, did that last week. My line manager is starting to get suspicious of my bimonthly bouts of diarrhoea and migraines. God, I hate work.

I drop my head between my legs – it's the only place it feels safe. It's dark under the bed. I remember when I was younger, running and leaping into bed terrified that something would jump out from that darkness and grab me. I'm not sure when I stopped doing that – but I do know I'm way too concerned with real life to worry about monsters nowadays.

II

46 minutes before

Five minutes later I've managed to get myself into an ill-fitting grey suit, off-white shirt and black tie and am dragging my feet down the steps at the front of my house. Damn, I need another shit. Have to put it out of my mind till I get to work now. I look down to Iffley Road. The traffic's moving quickly. I could go that way today rather than catching a bus on Cowley Road. On average it takes longer, but I'd quite like a break from my normal routine.

Christ, is that the time? I'll stick to the usual route. If I rush I may catch the 8.40.

It's cold. Apparently, it's going to be a bitter winter to complement the mild, rainy summer we've just had. Snow before Christmas they say, although that never turns out to be true. We'll probably just freeze and get no snow at all. I bet my boiler packs in again.

I cut through an overgrown church graveyard. The only sound is the crisp crunch of my steady pace on a grit-covered path. A huge green ocean of foliage washes through the place. Tightly packed crucifixes and gravestones stand like lighthouses of the underworld in the leafy waves. Many others have been swept beneath the plant life by the ever-flowing current of time. Stony echoes of lives lived drowning in unforgiving twisting thorns and thick bushels of grass. Older stones have even split as heavy-handed oak saplings grow from beneath. This boneyard is a true battlefield between nature and God; Mother Nature has wrapped her earthy fingers round this display of Middle Eastern Christianity and reclaimed it.

It's become a habit to acknowledge the gravestones on each side of the pathway. The names on each stone have become so familiar they feel like friends. Strange I know, but you take my point.

In Loving Memory of Madeline and Adam; *Rest in Peace Captain Peters*; *Loving Mother and Father, Betty and Bob*, and finally, *Here lies Annie Waits*. Annie always catches my eye. I can't help wondering what she's waiting for. She died young, just twenty-three, in 1943. Such an insignificant thing representing so much. A life of millions of words, glances and expressions all reduced to three impersonal lines. That's so depressing. *God*, I don't want to die. I bet Annie didn't want to die either. She can't say that on her gravestone, though, can she? I'd want it on mine. *Here lies Milton Pitt. He didn't want to die.*

There's an elderly man tending the grave. I see

him once a week maybe, always at Annie's grave only. 'Morning,' I greet.

'Give me a hand, boy?' he calls back with very little ceremony.

'Pardon,' I murmur, not quite catching the request.

'Give me a hand?' he grunts again.

'Um sorry,' I flounder, 'I'm already late.'

He says something else but I'm already too far away to hear. My heart always beats faster through this shortcut. Tramps and addicts use these huge, needled bushes as hideaways so I'm always a little edgy about pausing here. I breathe easier as the heather and brush open up and I leave the church's grand iron gates behind. Huge dark clouds are rolling over Oxford's jagged peaks, a contrast to the morning sun still warming my back. I walk the last block to the bus stop. The wind makes my eyes water, blurring the familiar mural of Cambodia's Angkor Wat on the wall of a local East Asian takeaway. Fleeing the coming storm, the low morning sun bounces from rooftop to rooftop, finding its way to a cricket pitch painted on one of the highest houses. Further on, white writing announces upcoming gigs at the Zodiac. No one of interest. It's a venue built in the true spirit of back-of-the-garage rock clubs; it's gross. From a simple house on Cowley Road it has grown organically over the years. Now, this over-evolved terrace embraces the nostalgic creatures of Oxford's rock underbelly like a beer-stained father.

Skipping down the long flight of concrete steps to my bus stop, I wonder if a little stumble would be enough to get me a day or two off work. Not a serious accident – I don't want to spend my day off in hospital – just enough of a gash to send me home with a tidy excuse. Then again, I hate pain as much as I hate work, so I may as well just go.

Damn, the 8.40 is coming. I'm going to have to run. I pick up my feet and propel myself through the bus's closing doors.

I climb to the top deck and drop into the first free seat. The dark clouds have obscured Cowley's morning skies. I watch large drops of rain hit the window.

A ticket inspector wobbles her way up to the top deck. She has a grey-dashed-brown bob haircut that competently frames a face tired and gaunt from too many years of dealing with the general public. With a uniform that's at least two sizes too big for her slim build, she shuffles down the aisle. Balls, what did I do with my ticket? Hastily, I start to rummage through my pockets; how have I got this many small pieces of paper? The inspector thanks the person ahead of me and turns in my direction. 'I've got it somewhere,' I say, checking my back pockets again. I've found a book of stamps, five receipts, two sweet wrappers and three old bus tickets, but I can't find the ticket I just fucking bought.

'What's your name?' she asks, readying herself to write up another fare-dodging chancer.

'Milton Pitt,' I answer absently, rifling through the many hidden areas of my wallet.

'Don't forget your top pocket, Mr Pitt.'

'I checked it,' I say with a suitable amount of contempt, dropping my hand into the pocket to prove it's empty. I pull out my ticket. Bollocks. 'Here you go, sorry.'

'Thank you, Mr Pitt,' she replies with a suitable amount of smugness.

The seats fill as we rattle down the road. I scan the strange and placid faces on the bus. Clumsily I make eye contact with a pretty girl in the reflection of the window and knee-jerk a smile before looking away. The man sitting two seats in front of me has an odd-shaped head. His wife's head, which he kissed goodbye at the last stop, was quite normal. Studying these cranial curves, I lose myself in God's flair for innovation. But I've probably been gazing into this crystal bald head for long enough. Back to scanning the bus, nothing much else to do.

A young mum, not bad looking, climbs the stairs, followed by a little girl, about three years old. Today's theme is obviously pink. Beneath her dark curls and big eyes is a puffy pink jacket, a bouncing pink tutu, frilly pink socks and little pink boots. She's ushered into the seat in front of me. Immediately, she jumps up and starts licking the window. Her mother doesn't notice – the germs are probably good for her anyway. At least it's keeping her quiet.

Next stop, another young mum, again not bad looking, accompanied this time by a boy, probably about the same age as the girl. His mother lags behind as he runs down the aisle. Both mothers have parenthood-worn grey complexions, like a good night's sleep is a thing of the past. The boy slows as he realises there aren't any seats left. 'Come here, Jack,' calls his mother, 'we'll sit downstairs.' I can tell this isn't going to go down well with Jack. The other mother can, too. She picks up her daughter, and slides across to make room for the little boy and his mother. The boy has what I expect is a long-dead Tamagotchi clenched between his teeth, the key chain hanging down like the tail of a mouse that's been caught by a cat.

The second mother smiles and sits. 'Thanks.'

'No problem,' replies the first. 'How old?'

The second young mother hauls her rather tubby son on to her lap. 'Just turned four. And yours?'

'Four in February.'

These few words are enough. They delve into their shared experiences of mystery rashes and chafed nipples, topics way off my radar. I lose interest.

Outside the window, the beaten-up buildings of Cowley have given way to the regal facades of Oxford's Colleges. Grandiose Gothic buildings appear one at a time through a thick mist brought on by the rain. Framed by grey, even the tiniest features are distinctive – gateways, bridges, trees, even the lamp posts feel like they've been here for ever. It's said that Oxford's old centre is crafted from the remains of Isis, a giant Egyptian goddess. Her dead skin hardened and formed the huge stone blocks used to construct Oxford's spires and statues. Bullshit anecdotes like this are tattooed to my brain. I made ends meet for a while working as a tour guide before I got my office job. I'm not sure which was worse. I got sacked pretty quickly anyway. The boss didn't like me telling the tourists that the University – and thus the city – is really just an ancient quango born from the overflowing pockets of men well versed in the subtle language of exploitation on a global scale. And that this gluttonous institution of the elite is an unstoppable juggernaut shepherding generations of fortunate alumni to their birth rights, and translating blazers and old boys to the highest overseas bidders. Plus I was drunk most of the time.

There's already a few groups of tourists knocking round – mostly Spanish students. They flood here every summer, and don't give a flying shit about the colleges, parks and museums. With all that young Latin blood coursing through their veins, all they do is drink and get into each other's underwear. I need to get more Spanish friends.

Glancing out of the front window, I realise my stop is next. That good old familiar uncomfortable feeling sinks through my body. I lean across to press the bell, but the second young mother beats me to it. The bus pulls up with a jolt, producing disgruntled moans from a few of the passengers. I wait for both mothers to gather their bags, coats and children and follow them downstairs. There's another pause as they retrieve their buggies, drag them off the bus and, with practised precision, effortlessly assemble them like a blindfolded soldier putting together his gun. I study them as I rummage through my bag for my door pass to the office. I'm always losing it – probably left it at home, again. I'll get a temporary. Crossing the quiet road between work and the bus stop, I find the two kids looking down at something. 'I think you two should stand on the pavement, don't you?' They look up. I wouldn't normally talk to strangers' kids, but I'm crossing the road anyway. '*Eek*. Is that a dead frog?' I blurt, as I spot the squashed amphibian they're studying on the tarmac.

'Yes,' replies the girl in a very matter-of-fact way.

The boy goes mute and scrunches his T-shirt. Obviously not comfortable talking to strangers – very sensible.

'Fog's eye's out,' the girl continues.

'So it is,' I reply, 'that's pretty horrific.' I sigh to myself, wondering how long this image will haunt me. 'Maybe you should go back to your mums.' I usher them to the pavement, gaining smiles of appreciation from the distracted, good-looking mums. Maybe one of them is a single mum. I smile and turn to cross the road.

...Bang...

Metal bumper. Legs ripped from beneath. Wild spin. Windscreen. Ricochet into the air. Suspended animation. Extend legs. Break fall. Pain sears. Legs shatter. My entire life crumbles to a single broken hallelujah in less than ten seconds.

...In...
I'll just close my eyes a minute.
...Out...
...

III

15 seconds after

What the hell? Must have passed out.

Feel strange. Weightless, numb, but no pain. Surely there should be pain?

I open my eyes. Not heavy or aching. There's a face, familiar... but... I've never seen it like this before. The eyes are glazed and unfocused like a mannequin. The lips are grey and blood runs from the nose. It's me! I'm looking down on my limp, lifeless body sprawled in the middle of the road. What's happening? Am I dying? I don't feel like I'm dying. What does dying feel like?

Must escape. I scream for my body to flee, but it won't. I'm paralysed, no, I'm floating. How am I floating? Like a puppet dangling on a string, I hang a foot above the ground, six inches from my gaunt, dying face. Face-to-face with myself.

There are shadows moving around my body. I

can't turn my head to see who's casting them and I'm too low to see anything more than shuffling feet.

'Can anyone hear me?' I call. 'Please, someone, help me!' But I already know the truth. I'm dying, and can't be heard by anyone.

Below me my white shirt is disappearing beneath a pool of thick red blood seeping from my chest. Must be where the car hit. My suit is ruined. That was an expensive suit. I must have slid at least six or seven metres before ending up here. Sides, elbows and legs have been shredded on the rough tarmac. I can even see deep burgundy patches of flesh through some of the tears.

A shrill siren cuts into my thoughts. Tyres screech to a halt. I'm moving, floating upwards. Still paralysed, I have no control over this horizontal ascent. I've already floated about a foot by the time two paramedics slide into the space I've created. There's a dark-haired man, in his forties judging by the spattering of grey hair. The other is a red-headed female, I'd guess she's no more than thirty. These details are far from certain as I can only see the tops of their heads. What I can say for sure is that the man has a ghastly dandruff problem and the woman a revealing pink bra. She should do a couple more buttons up when life-saving.

Quickly and efficiently they check my broken body's pulse on both my neck and arm. 'Pulse is very weak,' she says.

I have a pulse! I'm not dead! The man forces my

eyelids open and shines a bright torch directly into my pupils. 'Check for ID,' he instructs. Oddly, I can feel the heat of the torch on my face. How? If I'm up here and my body is down there? Maybe there's still a link between me and my body. Something flickers deep in my glazed eyes. A glimmer! I'm still in there. Maybe I don't have to die. 'Come on, you bastard! You can do it! Breathe, damn you, *breathe*!' I scream encouragement for my mortal body to live, and the glint in my eyes gets stronger. I feel myself being drawn back. I breathe deeply and prepare to delve back into the body I thought I'd lost. Praise the Lord, I'm going to live.

The woman rummages through my bag for a wallet. 'His name is Milton Pitt.'

The man takes hold of my chin. 'Milton, Milton, can you hear me? My name is Robert, you've been in an accident, I need you to look at me.'

'His vitals are dropping,' the woman reports.

'What?' I cry, alarmed by the noticeable concern. 'You're meant to save me.' I'm freaking out.

The woman interrupts my breakdown. 'We're losing him.'

I gaze deep into my own hazed eyes. 'Wake up. Wake up. Wake up. Breathe, you fucker! Wake up!' I scream.

'We'll have to resuscitate,' the man breathlessly states, 'clear his airways.'

Without warning, the glint disappears. I wail. 'No, where did I go? Come back! Wake up! Wake up, you bastard... let me back! I'm not ready to leave. Let me back in!' I watch myself die, receiving mouth to mouth from a sweaty forty-year-old man, slobbering and sprinkling dandruff all over my face. Why couldn't it have been the redhead?

I die. Not for any heroic or valiant reason, not to be a martyr, not to save the lives of loved ones, not to escape inner pain, not for belief, not for Queen or country, not realising dreams and not for my Juliet. No, I die because... why did I die? Poor road safety? Was the car speeding? It felt like it.

Like a ghostly flower I rise from the busy streets, passing praying angels and mourning gargoyles precariously balanced on the sides of the Colleges. I rise high enough to see the vehicle that hit me, a non-descript, three-door hatchback of some sort. It felt bigger. I look to my dead body. It's a strange thing to look at yourself without the use of a mirror or photograph. For twenty-six years that body has been my only viewpoint of the world, the medium for every sensation I've ever experienced and my whole idea of self. Now all I can do is float away.

To seal my fate, a cruel north wind catches me. I twist and spin in the breeze when all I want to do is scramble back and reclaim my body. But hard as I try, my inevitable progression is upwards. Like a drowning rat, I no longer have control of my destiny.

IV

36 minutes after

I feel like I'm losing my first and strongest love. 'So this is it, hey?' I mutter to myself like a gentle drunk. This is how it ends... lying in the middle of a rain-soaked road at my tender age without a single achievement to my damned name and nothing for people to remember a moment past my eulogy. On the positive side, at least the weather looks like it might be brightening up.

And then an unexpected realisation. *I've survived death.*

These words soar through me. I'm a superhero. No, I'm immortal. No, I'm a god. That shadow, that dark moment, that black-cloaked monkey on my back has passed without incident. Death, that ever-impending human condition that takes every one of us without exception, has passed me by on this winter's morning. Granted, I've clearly died – my corpse is proof of that – but here I am, still conscious, still aware.

Far from being a cataclysmic event, it's just another rather odd thing that has happened to me today. I've had a strange dream about a bald woman, watched a child lick a window, seen a frog with its eye out, punctured my heart and died. All in all, a rather odd morning. I breathe a sigh of relief. Like the passing of a worrying doctor's appointment or exam, I've got death out of the way and it didn't go too badly. Surprising how quickly the pain of death drains from your mind. Believe it or not, my entire body is fluttering with joy. I feel great.

This peace spreads to a tingling shiver as I soar above the rooftops. The wind whisks me in and out of university chimney pots and then, for no obvious reason, the blustering breeze drops and I'm floating above a skylight window-pane embedded in a slanted slate roof below. My movements are still in the hands of the gods (which ones I'm not sure) though. I'm paralysed.

Catching the reflection of myself, I realise I haven't considered the logistics of my sudden defiance of gravity. I'd just assumed weightlessness was a by-product of death. That's what they say, isn't it? Ascend to the next life, but this reflection suggests a surprising alternative. I can't see any detail in the window, but my darkened shape, silhouetted by the glistening sun through the soft cloud cover, isn't the shape or size I'd expected. Far from the Peter Pan-like figure I've been imagining, the shape I now cut against the morning sky is a mysterious creature a million miles from what I've woken up to for the last twenty-six years. What am I?

You might expect it to be distressing, the realisation that I've undergone substantial changes, but having seen my earthly body die, on some level I think I've let it go. Besides, the shock of watching my own death has probably left me heavily sedated. Staring deeper into my new form, I strain to see more than a silhouette. My face has definitely changed. It's constantly moving in ways I've never experienced. New senses vibrate through old ones, I have no idea what's going on. This is like puberty all over again. Oh well, it was always a very generic face, maybe a new one will bolster my wow factor. But what have I become?

As if in answer, the sun slides out from behind the clouds, casting gentle rays that illuminate my new form. I'm a butterfly.

My rhythmically beating wings light up like two glorious church windows. One by one, each perfectly positioned panel shines with sacred light.

And then I feel it. Starting as a gentle tingling, sensation flows through the vivid colours. I feel them beating. I feel their movement. I feel the power of the wind holding me in mid-flight. I become one with them, bonding them with the rest of my body, making it my own. I feel everything.

I've been reincarnated as a butterfly. Full metamorphosis. Is that a 'well done!' or a 'fuck you!' from the Big Man? It feels like a relegation. A bear or a dolphin

I could understand, but this seems harsh. I did call God a prick once. Although, since I had just lost my three fingers, you'd have thought they'd make allowances.

Hold on, if I'd truly been reincarnated as a butterfly I'd have the mind of a butterfly and couldn't possibly understand the concept of reincarnation. In fact, if I had been reincarnated as a butterfly, surely my thoughts wouldn't go further than fluttering and nectar. Are butterflies secret geniuses?

'What am I?' I question to two ends. Firstly, because I'm searching for an answer; and secondly, to prove to myself that while I have the body of a butterfly I still have the mental capacity of a human. It also strikes me that I shouldn't be speaking human English. Maybe I'm not, maybe I'm speaking butterfly. No, it definitely sounds like English. But how would I know? Maybe my interspecies transformation comes with an inbuilt translator. Makes sense that if I'm a butterfly I'll be able to communicate with other butterflies. I hope I don't have to learn it; I'm awful at languages.

Those wings are mighty pretty – maybe it is a promotion. Can't argue that I was a long way from beautiful in human form, but now I'm stunning. A body that natural selection has tailored generation by generation for one single purpose: to radiate pure, untainted attraction. I wonder if I'm meant to mate with other butterflies. Not sure I fancy butterflies. Which ones are the females? God, I'm confused. I'll just hope for the best.

I flutter my wings and brace myself against a passing gust. The breeze whisks my three-gram frame from the window and sends me spinning into the air. I beat once, then again, and the third time comes as naturally as breathing.

I suppose that now I'm an insect I should start living the life of one. No job, no more angst, no more bus journeys and no more clothes – this might not be too bad. The wind propels me at speed but there's time to glance back to Earth. Or, more precisely, to my earthly remains, which are still holding up traffic. The paramedics have lifted me on to a stretcher and covered my face with a white sheet. They're surrounded by inquisitive accountants wondering if this experience is harrowing enough to excuse them from work today. The woman who'd been driving the car is slumped on the pavement, her head in her hands. She's on the phone to somebody, probably trying to explain what has happened to a friend or relative.

Nothing else to do. I may as well flutter down and take a look at the person God has deemed fit to end my life. I duck under a street light and, taking advantage of this abundance of hot air, I glide through the curious crowds until, glancing along the busy pavement, I see her. I approach. A few metres away I hesitate. She is my angel of death after all, the person whose soul God has fatally intertwined with my own.

I cautiously lower myself onto her knee. My touch is so light she doesn't notice. Her hair is dyed the lighter shade of blonde and is tied up in a knot. Slim cheeks rise from a thick black scarf that rests on a long, grey herringbone overcoat. It slits half-buttoned into a pair of charcoal suit trousers and high heels. Like a climber bracing against a cliff-face she digs the points of the heels into the tarmac.

Bitter thoughts rumble through the winding favelas of my mind until they reach an unexpected place: a reason for my death. Unbeknown to her, this woman could have the unrealised potential to be someone great. She could have the potential to educate, liberate, even save the lives of millions and to unleash it. All that was needed was a little nudge. My death could already be the first link in a chain of events leading this woman to something truly world-altering.

Having rested these monumental ideals on my killer's shoulders, all the blame and malice I have for her drains away. Even though her weepy eyes are closed, I see beauty there. 'So you're the one that ended me,' I say, words that she, of course, doesn't hear or comprehend, but it helps me. And she is beautiful. Easily beautiful enough to save the world. From this day forth, I will be her angel, as she has been mine. I will flutter with her, sit on her shoulder whispering words of inspiration until one day she will repay my sacrifice by fulfilling her potential and helping, nay saving, humanity. Caught up in the moment, I beat my wings with joy. She opens her eyes.

'You see me,' more silent butterfly words escape.

Squinting, she moves closer, silently inspecting me. She stares deep into my bulging butterfly eyes and I stare straight back. Her eyes are vast, the colour of the clearest blue skies. I've never exchanged meaningful glances with a creature fifty times my size before. It's exhilarating... yet terrifying. Her lips quiver, about to speak... then pause. 'It's okay. Speak... to me,' I invite. She hears nothing.

Her lips quiver again. 'What do you mean my insurance won't cover this?' she snarls at the anonymous phone operator. Immediately, she loses all interest in me, her focus back on her phone. Dark clouds roll over her sky-blue eyes as her mood turns blacker than night. Her voice wails like a dentist's drill. She doesn't sound very humbled at all.

My gallant reason for dying is under threat.

Her brows crash together. 'Look, you spineless, money-grabbing piss fruit,' she sneers, 'I've got a dented bonnet, scratched paintwork and a broken windscreen, and there's no way I'm paying for it. That's what my insurance is for. Why else would I pay it? I might as well not bother.' A pause as the voice on the phone attempts to explain something. 'It wasn't my fault,' she interrupts, 'he ran straight out in front of me.'

Oh God, she's the anti-Christ. She doesn't even care that she's killed me! She ended everything I had the potential to be: a loving husband, father, someone who could make a mark on the world, and all she's concerned about is her fucking windscreen.

'What do you mean after the last time,' she snaps. 'That wasn't my fault either, the cyclist wasn't paying attention... of course I had to pick up my phone... it was making a strange sound... put me on to your boss.'

She's killed before! I'm the victim of a mass murderer. How could I not see it? *Those eyes*. How did I miss those eyes? They're pure evil. There's nothing there, no regret, no remorse, not even a damn tear.

She's looking at me again.

She wouldn't.

Don't you...

What a bitch.

V

1 hour 2 minutes after

Everything is dark and everything is quiet.

She squashed me. She actually squashed me. As if hitting me with her car wasn't enough, she squashed me with her bare hands! Who kills a butterfly with their *bare hands*? My lips curl with anger. Lips? Human lips? I grab my face. I'm alive. And I'm not a butterfly.

I open my two human eyes. 'Where am I?' I'm groggy. It takes a few moments to focus... on... my bedroom ceiling? I'm home, lying in my bed... how the fuck? Peeking under the sheets, I check my hands, legs, feet and every other extremity that confirms I am, indeed, human. I'm definitely not a butterfly. Thank fuck for that! I rub my arms – I've never been so happy to have all my limbs in the right place.

Was it just a dream? Goddamn I've had some freaky dreams this morning. Strange bald girls, death, being turned into an insect... what did I eat last night? Hangover dreams maybe. Speaking of which, my hangover seems to have gone. *Result*. Must've slept it off.

I run the sensitive stubs of my three little fingers through my hair. I actually really enjoy the sensation. It feels clean. How can it be? I draw in the room's cool air. Mint? My teeth are clean. Must be a trick of the mind. The booze has probably messed with my senses.

Better get up, I'm probably late for work. I could pull a sicky. No, did that last week... Wow... déjà vu.

I stretch out in the bed and run my eyes round the room. Everything is as it was in my dream. I have my T-shirt and black tracksuit bottoms on and the smell of sick from my bin is still overpowering.

The clock's off – no display. That's different. I push buttons randomly and give it a tap – nothing. I hit it harder. Still nothing. Damn clock. How late is it?

The telly is on. Same as my dream: Teletext channel, Spurs 2 Liverpool 1, and *X-Files* is sticking out of the video player. I guess I watched it so I dreamt about it. Forcing myself out of bed, I stumble to the wardrobe. As I've already dressed myself in the dream, the choice is easy. Shirt, tie... where's my grey suit? Did I take it to the cleaners?

With blue suit in hand I turn, and then I see them. My breath stops. My heart stops. My suit drops. It feels like I'm being watched from every shadow. I'm trapped, confused, can't move. I would jump back into bed but I'm terrified that something might actually grab me. Am I still asleep? Am I still dreaming? It shouldn't surprise me after the morning I've had. I dig my nails into my skin to make sure this time. Nothing changes. I'm awake. How can I be seeing this?

Slowly and silently I press my back against the wardrobe. I cough to try to make it feel real. It doesn't. Leaning forward, I touch the red trail on my sheet. It's cold. I smell it. My dream! It smells the same as the blood in my dream. My blood. I haven't had much experience... have I?... But if this isn't blood it's a pretty good substitute. What is going on? If I lived in a shared house I'd say this was a really dark practical joke. But I don't. I live alone.

I shake my head, but they're still here. Bloody footprints tracing a path across my white duvet and off the end of the bed. Tiny, bloody footprints. Something has walked across the bed while I was asleep, stopped by my head and walked away. And for some reason (probably not a healthy one), it had blood on its feet.

Breathe... calm down.

The footsteps continue across the floor and then disappear up the chimney of my bedroom fireplace. Thank God, at least it's not hidden somewhere in the room. They look like miniature human prints. Is there an injured child up there? I fall silent, listening for any kind of sound. Nothing. Can't be, these aren't the fat little feet of a toddler; they're slim. The stride isn't right either. The prints are too precise, too controlled. A kid that small wouldn't be able to walk so steadily, would they?

Stepping in and out of the bloody prints, I fix my eyes on the suspiciously quiet fireplace. All thought of going to work is forgotten as I trace the red-stained route up the back and out of sight. Caution feels wise. Picking up my shaving mirror, I angle it to inspect the flue. At first all I see is bricks and soot. But then a few more splashes of blood, and, further up the shaft, a dim glow cutting across the darkness. The solitary light is too localised to be cast downwards by the morning sun; it must be coming from somewhere else. I lower myself backwards to inspect the chimney. Looking closer, I'm able to make out a metre-wide hole in the back. More bloody prints illuminated by the light disappear into it. There's no way an injured child could get up there. So what?

My neighbour on this side is Mr Lennon, a widowed seventy-eight-year-old who sometimes invites me in for tea. This must lead directly into his bedroom. Does he know about this? Has he been through here? It could be something innocent; he could be injured.

I should probably call the police, but what if he is injured? I need to check it out.

Carefully, I stand up inside the chimney. It's tight. 'Christ,' I hiss, catching my shoulder on the corner of a brick. Inch by inch, I squeeze my way to the opening. I can't believe this is here! How have I never noticed it before? If I've judged it right, my head should be directly in line with the base of the opening. I glance in. There is a room on the other side; but it's not an old man's bedroom. Far from it. What is going on? Where is this? Did I get turned around? The first thing my slowly adjusting eyes see is a wood-panelled wall, followed by an ornate ceiling decorated with elaborate gold leaf.

The room is vast, an immense ballroom. I see halfway across before a claustrophobic murk becomes too thick to penetrate. There's no natural light; instead of windows, there are two grand chandeliers holding candles that are illuminating piles of... what... what looks like treasure. 'My God!' I exclaim.

A strange glow floating like a lighthouse on a distant rocky outcrop gives me an idea of the room's length. This definitely isn't Mr Lennon's place – the room is bigger than his entire house – so where is it? I'm going in.

I scan for any movement, in particular for the owner of the bloody feet. Nothing. Poking my head through the hole, I can see more. 'Bloody hell.' All kinds of treasures and artefacts are stacked in front of me: marble statues, portraits, dozens of elegantly crafted musical instruments, heavily jewelled crowns, swords of all shapes and sizes, huge, gold-framed mirrors and an enormous stuffed grizzly staring directly at me with vicious glass eyes.

I listen intently, but only silence hangs in the dusty air, as does a line of shrunken heads.

Leaning awkwardly into the opening, I edge forward. There's something below the hole; a soft fabric. Levering my head further through, I make out a luxurious red carpet framed by a spiralling golden banister. With a final push I spill out of the chimney and tumble down the ornate staircase into a suit of armour, sending it crashing to the ground. I freeze, waiting to be discovered. Nothing. After a few moments I breathe again, ease the heavy breastplate from my body and look back at the hole. On this side the red-carpeted staircase leads to a metre-high door fitted neatly into the panelled wall and decorated with weathered brass fittings, including an oversized circular handle.

I drag the remaining armour from my legs and stumble to my feet, uncovering an impressive sword. It's light, but even with minimal pressure the razor-sharp end cuts into the well-polished floor as I run the steely point across the hardwood grain. Perfect for defending myself, if necessary. I listen again, then tentatively follow the bloody trail between two looming towers of relics.

With heavy breath I weave my way into this manmade maze. I feel like an explorer discovering a tomb, anticipating traps round every corner. The alleyways grow narrow as I push deeper. The piled-high relics make it almost impossible for the little light the candles cast to sneak into these tight passages.

At each taxidermied beast, Egyptian sarcophagus or flamboyant piece of furniture, my heart beats faster. What if I have to use this sword? I've no idea what I'm doing. Where are these footprints leading... um... they're... um... My thoughts crumble. They've stopped, in the middle of the passage, just stopped, dead. I wipe my sleeve round the nape of my clammy neck. I feel very exposed. 'Fucking relax,' I advise myself, 'there's a logical explanation.' I focus on the artefacts, seeing everything and nothing. With every sense heightened to bursting I cautiously study the final pair of footprints. What happened? I scan the crates. No blood, but there's a discarded rag on one of them. I stab it with my sword and lift for a closer inspection. It's covered in red liquid. Whatever made these prints must have noticed the blood trail and wiped its feet. This is not an injured party. I don't know what to think, so I try not to.

With a flick of the sword I fling the bloody rag onto a small crate a few metres away. My heart stops. Next to it is a book I recognise. The cover shows a single woman leaning gracefully over a balcony, a Cuban woman with well-worn clothes and messy hair that speak of poverty, but not a sad, down-trodden poverty; rather, a bewitching, raw, Latin poverty. It's *Pictures of Cuba*, my *Pictures of Cuba*! Even without opening it, I know it's mine. The scuffs round the edge are unmistakable. Holding it close I even get the faint odour of last night's vomit. Was it gone when I woke up? I shake my head. What is going on? Why would someone steal my book? Someone with bloody feet. There's no good answer. I've gone far enough. I'm breaking and entering into a psychopath's house. I'm in over my head. I should go back through the little door and call the police.

I hear a noise. Instinctively glancing towards it, I spot a black shape hidden deep in a small tunnel beneath another pile of crates. Its eyes shine white in the darkness. Our stares lock, then with little tapping footsteps, it vanishes. In a burst of adrenaline, I dive towards the hole and squeeze between the crates on elbows and knees just in time to see a creature disappear round a corner ahead of me. 'What the hell is that?' I exclaim. The crates create a tunnel through the debris, like the White Rabbit's warren winding deep into the piles of treasures. I bang against the rough boxes as I scramble down the passage, taking agonising seconds to crawl to the first corner. It's there for a second, then gone. This corridor is tighter, but I force my way along, the walls compressing me until I'm lying flat to the ground.

'What the hell are you doing, Milton?' I voice my concerns out loud. 'This is insane.' I peer round the next corner. The corridor's even longer and empty. These tunnels must penetrate all the piles in the room. I could still turn round – but I don't. I'd go back to my room, and then what? Wait? I need to know what it is.

It's small, that I do know. I think I'd have the edge. I crawl past the feet of statues and under antique chairs. I turn another corner... and this time, at the far end, it's waiting for me. Staring straight at me. I freeze, waiting for its next move.

In the stillness I become aware of a glow from behind the creature. The soft light defines its outline. It's human... and male, the size of a three-year-old, but definitely not a child. 'Who are you?' I shout. He doesn't answer, just breathes, gruff and laboured. Something spooks him; he turns and runs. As he does, the strange glow picks out a small white loincloth; the rest of him as nature intended, including a big bushy beard. I don't understand. He came into my room with bloody feet, took my book as some kind of weird memento and now he's... what? Timid?... Unless it's a trap. I scramble down the tight pathway, press myself against a wall and fumble the sword from my belt. I thrust the sharp point into the blind space round the next corner. Nothing.

I peer round. The passageway spills out into what looks like the other end of the room. What do I do? I'll be defenceless if I crawl out. I scrutinise the area. The creature's nowhere to be seen. It's got to be done. Making as little noise as possible, I edge into position, get a sure footing on two sturdy crates, then propel myself forward, breaking free of the tunnel blindly swinging the sword.

I open my eyes. Nothing, apart from a pool of blood seeping beneath me. Hard to miss, it's everywhere. Looks like he's gutted someone right here on this floor. He's a psycho and he's out for blood.

VI

1 hour 47 minutes after

Soaked in blood, I stumble to my feet. Can't see the little savage anywhere, but what I do see is far, far worse. Sitting slashed and mutilated in the blood is a fresh heart. I'm going to vomit... or pass out. But I can't. Got to keep my wits about me. The little bastard is here somewhere. Probably plotting my untimely death. I consider escaping back to my room again, but the only choice is an unstable wall of artefacts or the tunnel. Neither appeals. Why did I come here?

I poke the heart with my sword. Is it human? In the middle of the pool is a low stone table, its strange carvings all soaked in blood. Can't be long since the sick ritual was performed right here.

To the left of the fireplace is a red leather chair and a mahogany desk with matching red leather topping. But it's not the lavish trimmings that make this desk noteworthy – it's the size. Both are crafted to the man's mini dimensions, and the custom fittings don't stop there. A suitably sized gold-tinted typewriter sits on the desk. I try to lift it. It may be small but it's heavy. Solid gold?

Beside the typewriter are four gigantic piles of paper, illogically balanced over three metres high. The pages are quarter-size, like large post-it notes. What was he writing?

I check under the desk and in the drawers. Nothing of note. I place the sword on the desk and, via all fours, cautiously stand on the surface. Reaching up I grab a handful of sheets from the top of the pile. I hear a voice. I freeze.

From behind the paper mountain I hear him – the fireplace! He's up the chimney. Why didn't I think of that? I've already followed him up one chimney today.

Stuffing the papers into my trouser pocket, I slip off the table, pick up the sword and move towards the fireplace. A thick trail of blood leads from the fire, across the fireplace, and is smeared all the way to the table. With a fire burning it's impossible for anybody to get up there, but I can still hear the voice. I search the crevices and alcoves, but no little psycho bastard in sight. Maybe I've scared him off.

I slump down, my back pressed against the wall – I'd like to see him sneak up on me here. I consider my options. Option 1: get the fuck out. That seems to be it. But how? Where to? Paralysed by indecision, I sense the fire getting hotter. In seconds it's grown to a raging inferno barely contained by the fireplace. More than that, I see shapes, not of wood or dancing flames, but people, becoming clearer as I stare. I gasp as I recognise a familiar face in the flames. I hear the voice again. It's Hattie Harris.

The voice wasn't the creature. It's unmistakably Hattie, a maternal forty-something who sits across from me at work. I've worked with Hattie at Taylor, Smith and Plump for two years. We don't have much in common but our enforced eight-hour cohabitation has fostered a kind of understanding. She talks about her three kids, car and husband; I talk about my unhealthy lifestyle, hamster and romantic interests, or lack thereof. On those feeble foundations we've learnt to co-exist. I've no idea what Hattie does and suspect she has no idea what I do, but as my current job description can be summed up as writing and receiving emails to and from arseholes five days a week, there's no loss there.

'Hattie. Hattie. Hattie Harris,' I say in hushed tones to the fire. 'Can you hear me?' She doesn't. Moving closer, I see she's sitting at her desk, but the focus isn't on her, it's on my empty desk across from her, laid out exactly as I left it yesterday, computer and monitor in the middle with my mug and water bottle on one side, in-tray and stationery on the other. Hattie sits on the other side of the partition as she always does, with only her bright red lips, big glasses and tightly curled hair poking above the divide. My God, this little stalker has been spying on me at work. The freak. But how can I see the image in the flames? Some sort of projection? I wave across the front of the fire. But the image doesn't alter. How's he doing it? I stare at Hattie. She's talking on the phone. Straining, I listen.

'I don't know who it was. Could have been someone in the building,' Hattie gossips in that monotone, matter-of-fact voice of hers. 'I only really saw the ambulance driving away.' I bet she's talking to Brenda, her overweight friend in HR. 'I know, Brenda, they're always speeding along that road, it was just a matter of time. Well, keep me updated.' She puts the phone down.

My stomach sinks. An accident... outside the office... this morning... my dream... was it a dream? As my mind ticks from thought to thought Hattie's phone rings again. 'Good morning, Taylor, Smith and Plump. Hattie Harris speaking.' She examines her nails as the caller introduces themselves. 'I see. How can I help, Officer?' The tone of her voice suggests she is about to be privy to some grade A gossip. Her expression freezes, then the slightest of glances towards my chair. 'Yes, he works here, but he's not at his desk at the—' She stops dead. 'Today, outside? I heard something had happened,' she wobbles. 'How is he?' A broken gasp. 'I understand. Thank you. Goodbye.' I'm only inches from the fire, close enough to see the colour drain from her cheeks. Her watery eyes stare down at the phone.

'What did they say?' I demand of the flames. 'Tell me what they said.'

We both wait in silence. Hattie's head slowly

rises to gaze at my vacant office chair. Tears stream from beneath her glasses. I understand now. Slowly, Hattie's hand fumbles towards her phone. 'Brenda, it's Hattie. The police just called... it's about Milton,' she sniffs. 'Yes, Milton Pitt, who sits across from me. It was him that got knocked down.' Her jaw tightens as Brenda speaks. 'No. Dead. Died right there.' She puffs to control her breathing. 'I know, young.' Brenda asks another question. 'I don't know, I guess I'll just go home. Can't be here.' The fire fades to a quiet burn and Hattie disappears.

I slump to my knees; my hands impact hard on the slate surface to break my fall. 'I'm...' I can't bring myself to say it.

'Dead,' comes a sharp voice from behind. He's crept up on me! Twisting to my left, I grab for the sword but freeze as something sharp presses against the back of my neck. 'Don't,' he hisses. 'I am an expert in eight forms of swordsmanship, and you, Milton Pitt, have a B-Tech in cookery, so leave the sword where it is.'

How does he know that?

He breaks his own silence, 'Shush, I'll ask the questions.'

A whimper escapes my lips. 'I didn't say anything.'

'Not you,' he jabs, 'them.'

'Who?' I snivel.

'I don't know how he got here,' he snaps. 'He could have found the door by himself,' he continues.

'I don't know... he may have happened to look up the chimney. What did you say?' he demands. 'No you're a moron... no you're a moron... no you are a... enough. I will ask him... I will... I will... Silence... Shut up!'

Who's he talking to? Oh God, he's fucking crazy. A moment of stillness.

'Did you follow my footprints?' Is he talking to me? I yelp as he prods me. 'Did you?' he demands.

'Ye-es,' I stutter.

He tuts rapidly. It's very menacing. 'You should *not* have done that. No, no, no, this is bad. I know it's bad.'

'I didn't say anything,' I repeat.

'I know we need to get rid of him.'

'Oh God, I'm sorry,' my voice peaks, 'I'll just go. Please let me go.'

'Quiet, Milton,' he demands through tight teeth.

I obey. I feel his eyes on me. Examining me like a piece of meat.

'I've never seen one in real life, and conscious,' he rapidly continues.

'Please don't kill me,' I blurt.

'Why would we kill you?' he snips. '...What do you mean, we could? How?... No, you can't beat him to death with a rock... I know we have plenty, that's not the point. It's rude.' He speaks with manic intensity now. 'Well, I'd swiftly detach his C3 and C4 cervical vertebrae, but that's just me, I'm kind like that... I know, like cutting butter. Calm yourself,' he hisses, 'I know you're a proud man, but he is our

guest and you will treat him as such... you will...
yes, you will... ah okay... go on then if you're so
proud.'

My heart stutters. 'Go on what?' I gripe.

'This doesn't involve you, Milton,' he dismisses.
'Kazuo has a point to prove, apparently.'

'It sounds like it's to do with me,' I say, glancing
left then right.

'Well, it's not. Trust me.' Hooking his little
hand under my chin, he presses the blade harder,
and says, 'If Kazuo wants to kill you then that's his
issue, not yours.'

'What?' I gasp.

The moment hangs in the air. 'Ha!' he barks. 'I
knew it! I knew you didn't have the guts to do it...
you're more chicken than him... at least he picked
the sword up... that's right, back to your corner...
I'm sorry about that.' He pats the back of my head.
'It would have been a pointless exercise anyway, you
being dead and all.'

I bring myself to ask the question: 'I'm really
dead?'

'Are you joking? Is he joking? You still think
you're alive?' He pauses. I feel the tip of the blade
give a little. 'Yes, you're dead. You got hit by a car
and now you're dead,' he informs me as if it's a great
inconvenience. '...I don't think he does. Surely you
remember?'

Numb, my head tilts. 'Well, yes, but I thought...'
I turn a little. 'So... not a dream?'

'No, not a dream,' he whispers agitatedly, 'your death, from your earthly life in any eventuality.'

Even though this is the strangest of statements, from the strangest of sources, in the strangest of places, somehow I know this creepy little man is telling the truth. Somewhere inside I already feel far from my old life. Too far to return.

With the courage of someone who is already condemned, I turn to face my little assailant. On my knees I look right into his eyes. He's even smaller than I thought, no taller than half a metre. He has the exact dimensions of an average-sized human – just a third of the size. His skinny body and loincloth are hidden beneath a thick red cloak hanging from his shoulders. It reflects the shimmering flames in the fireplace in a way I've never seen before, as though the cloak is on fire itself. It casts light up to the man's thick ginger beard. His look falls somewhere between a homeless garden gnome and a traffic cone. Matted clumps of hair hang down, a busy, grease-mangled jungle contradicting the face semi-hidden below. It's not old and withered as the rest of his appearance would suggest, but the face of a young man at the peak of his strengths, about my age. His eyes are bright and his skin unwrinkled, although he's jittery, and has significant facial tics.

'What?' The erratic man demands. I'm obviously not hiding my shock very well.

I drop backwards onto the fireplace and exhale slowly. 'I really am dead.' Death is easier to accept this time round. I've already done it once today. 'The butterfly,' I blurt out. 'Surely the butterfly was a dream.'

His stare is piercing. Eyes fixed on my face. Not on my eyes, though, on my features; every time my brow furrows or lips move his eyes are on them. There's more – this examination seems to be linked to his hand. Every look is accompanied by a strange movement in the fingers. It's like the hand not holding his sword is constantly playing an invisible piano. It's weird.

I study him studying me. A crooked snigger escapes his mouth. 'No, you didn't turn into a butterfly. This is the Afterlife, not Narnia.' In one fluid motion he sheathes the sword into a walking cane with an echoing snap. 'Forget about the butterflies; they're not important.' Silence. His eyes jerk right, but oddly his head doesn't move. It's as if he hears something from behind but doesn't dare look. 'No, they're not. It's just a dream!' He's talking to someone again. I search the area behind him as subtly as possible. It's empty. He's crazy. 'He would never have found out if he didn't get lost.' He continues to listen to someone with the frustration of a nagged husband. 'No... no... no... okay! I'll tell him... yes, sorry.' His eyes shoot back to me, seemingly fearful of missing even the slightest expression in my face. Fingers still dancing, he releases the pressure in his jaw with a long breath from his nostrils. 'Your butterfly dream was a dream, and a very important dream at that.

It is a state of unconsciousness crafted by nature. No different to the way it has crafted the apple or the fat American. Completely natural. It's a temporary condition through which every human passes to two ends. Firstly,' – he jabs his cane into my chest – 'it's nature's anaesthetic to the significant and traumatic changes your physical body goes through in and after death. But a simple painkiller is nothing; even you humans have discovered those. It's the second end in which we see the true harmonies of Mother Nature's poetry.' He pauses again to be certain of my full attention. 'This dream-suspended condition is not only a funeral carriage to the other side, it is mental preparation. It understands what you need for a smooth transition into the Afterlife and finds the perfect way to deliver it. For you it was butterflies. Do you know what I mean?'

Even holding the cane, both hands now float in the air, playing the invisible piano. It's difficult to ignore. 'I think I do.' I simply answer, remembering how gently that dream led me from my earthly death to this acceptance. I've actually come to terms with my passing. 'It's a hell of a dream.'

'It is.' His wild eyes twitch right then left, still without his head moving. 'What do you mean *the whole thing*? That is the *whole thing*.' He tries to ignore the unseen party. 'Yes... I'm sorry... I'm sorry... okay... sorry.' They apparently won't be ignored. 'Okay! I'll finish it, just shut up, I can't hear my own thoughts!' his voice echoes in the hall.

He composes himself. 'Not a single detail will have been missed,' he emphasises to the empty space beside him, then looks back to me. 'Every aspiration, desire, taste, disservice or insult,' – each of these words has a related action – 'is coerced into the realisation that you are dead. For every human this insight is the same and every dream different. Some subjects dream of past relations gently whispering *it's going to be okay*, others have a one-to-one with their God on a cloud somewhere, and for you, well, it involved butterflies, and being killed a second time just to hammer the point home.' He grunts as his eyes travel right. 'No, I don't think anyone has ever needed to die twice to get the message – our Milton Pitt is one of a kind.'

'So,' I try to grasp my current reality, 'reincarnation isn't real?'

'God no, we can't go round turning people into animals – it's just not ethical. Anyway, what would be the point? They wouldn't know the punishment – they'd just trot around doing animal stuff.'

'I guess so,' I sniff.

'What about the bitch who killed me? I got that right, didn't I?' I state with more confidence.

'Who do you think killed you?' He stifles a mocking grin.

'That evil young woman, with the cheekbones, and the dyed blonde hair, and the thick black scarf, and the overcoat, she was a nightmare.' The words still leave a bitter taste.

'Well, congratulations, Milton, you're also a sexist pig.'

'What? I'm not!' I dumbly protest.

'Don't blame yourself. Things change quickly; in the 1930s you would have been seen as progressive.'

'I'm not sexist!' I protest slightly louder.

'Calm yourself, Milton, you've nothing to prove in this place,' he dismisses.

My mouth forms to speak again, but before I can he continues. 'That bitch that murdered you.'

'Yeah?'

'Was a sixty-year-old man.' His voice slows a little. I think he's beginning to forget his rush and to enjoy mocking me.

'But I saw her,' I mutter with less conviction.

'That part of your dream was way off!' he indulges himself. 'You did see him.' He jabs one of his tiny dancing fingers in my direction. 'I know because I saw him, but you were in a death roll so I'll forgive you not remembering, and instead your *non*-sexist mind dreamt up your best stereotypical mental image of a bad driver, which apparently is a twenty-something woman.'

My expression rotates to confusion.

'Don't worry yourself, Milton,' he snorts. 'Ay,' he directs back to the left and grunts agreement, 'you may well be right, he is a horny little bastard. He did sexualise as well as stereotype her after all. Don't worry yourself about it. It's the second death we can't believe.' He startles me with a loud shriek and wheels away. 'That's it. That's why he woke early! The second time the woman killed him, she woke him prematurely from the dream.' He bounces the end of the cane on the floor. 'This is fantastic news! The bloody footprints, the waking early... his fault, not mine. My record is clean.' He completes a circle and locks eyes back with me with a long self-congratulatory exhale. 'So,' he asserts, 'you're probably currently wondering, what next? What is this place? Who am I? And perhaps how I know your name, Milton Pitt.'

'Well,' my eyes narrow, 'yes.'

His eyes flit to the right. 'Yes, such bland questions,' he agrees with someone as his unflattering grin turns to a thoughtful grimace. 'Well, he might as well take a seat if he's staying to the end.' Without taking his stare from me he backs away and directs me to the small chair behind the desk. Clambering to my feet, I feel like a giant. I shake my leg to get the blood flowing, and then wedge myself in the tiny leather chair. He rubs his face in an attempt to stir himself. 'To answer your dull questions, I have no idea, this is the Afterlife – specifically the residence of the Narration, I am a Narration, I am one of many Narration. More than that, I know you, Milton Pitt, because I am your Narration.' His speech is finally a little softer. There's the hint of a familiar accent. I can't place it. 'Every human has a Narration,' he continues, 'there isn't a person on Earth that doesn't have one looking over them right now, chronicling each and every move.' Extending a cloaked arm towards my shadow, the Narration punctuates this sentiment. 'From the shadows we Narration watch the greatest triumphs and saddest lows of our assigned wards.'

'You're my Narration,' I say, sounding out the concept. 'Strange name.'

'Functional, though,' he shoots back, 'does what it says on the tin.'

'I guess so.' This small chair is pinching. I squirm. 'And I'm your ward?'

'Yes, every move, we've been there.'

I consider what he's seen. '*Every move?*'

'We've seen that look before.' He sniggers to the right. 'Don't be bashful. Watched hundreds of men and women over the ages experiment with their bodies in all manner of ungodly ways. So, your 852 masturbations and... what?' His eyes jerk right. 'Ah yes, right you are, Arik-boke. Actually, 853: you had a drunken one last night, you dirty bastard, and twelve sexual encounters is nothing, trust me.'

I'm too stunned at the detail of these statistics to even question how he, or Arik... um... whatever, can recall how many times I've self-completed. 'For the last twenty-six years we've studied your every twitch, glance and tremble. Sitting in that very chair, we watched your first kiss, watched those three fingers of yours get slammed in that car door and watched in awe as you somehow pooed in your own trouser pocket on holiday in Spain.'

I gape. 'I remember that. I was young.'

'You were four,' he speaks instantly, 'and even if I live to narrate on another 568 lives I'll never forget the first time you took drugs and got in a fight with that Yorkshire Terrier. It was the moment you turned to that Korean friend of yours and told him, "I don't like the way that dog's looking at me." Then the next thing we know you're rolling round on the floor with it like you're in the Wild West. Damn funny.'

His accent breaks through again as he laughs. It's like an itch I can't scratch – why is it so familiar? I can't help but smirk too. 'Nope, no memory of that. I do remember the pain the morning after. You know everything then?'

He wipes a tear from his eye and straightens up. 'I can safely say, Milton Pitt, that we know you better than you know yourself.'

I suddenly recall the terror my so-called Narration caused me on my way in here. 'If you know me so well, why run from me in the tunnel? Why stick a sword in my back?'

His eyebrows peak. 'Because I do know you, is why. What would you have done with that sword?'

'I don't know,' I say honestly.

He leans in to hold my stare. 'I do. You're a frightened person, you always have been, and if I know one thing about humanity, and more importantly about you, Milton Pitt, it's that you do not underestimate a frightened person. Especially when cornered and within reach of a blade. You could have caused me serious harm. Though more than likely it would have been the other way round. Neither option appealed, so I applied the exact pressure for an outcome agreeable to us both. Played you like a fiddle, my boy.' He glares for an intimidating second, then softens. 'Although, that did surprise me.'

'What?'

'You didn't turn tail and run the moment you saw me. That was far braver than I gave you credit for – death suits you.'

I try to hold my bravado. 'Wouldn't have been my first fight.'

'Your boxing.' He smirks to the right. 'Didn't stop you being frightened, though, did it? Taught you how to protect yourself, but also all the ways people can hurt you; always just one punch away from permanent brain damage. No, if anything it made you worse. Made you timid. Shame, with the right attitude you could have been good.' The hairy markers of expression on his face leap. 'We love you when you're wasted. Your brawl last night in the pub was beautiful, that's the Milton we love watching. Arik-boke almost popped a nut he shouted so loud.'

The Narration's skilled eyes dart round my face. I don't feel I'm showing my discomfort, but his mirrored frown suggests it's there. 'Don't beat yourself up. Not your fault. It's your society,' he attempts to console. 'The great global network where everyone knows everything instantly,' he hails. 'How could you not be scared with the world's horror stories served up to you every night with your microwave dinner? I've watched it all. From the shrieks of early ape-man, smoke signals, drums, semaphore, radio, video recorders, television, satellites, mobile phones, email, the internet. It all happened *way* too fast for you humans. You barely have the mental capacity to deal with your own problems, let alone what the world dishes up. No wonder your fuzzy little brains retreat and expect death round every corner. And why do you do it to yourselves?' he barks.

I don't have a fucking clue – and he knows it.

'Politics 101? Keep you living in fear? No, too obvious. Much simpler than that. You humans find it entertaining.' He waggles the cane at me and then raises his hands to the ceiling. 'You still yearn to hear ape-man shriek.'

'Okay, okay,' I finally cut in as he catches his breath, 'you're right. I was terrified. Happy?'

'I know you were.' This seems to appease him. 'I like talking to you, Milton. Strange that. Thought you'd be too... basic, I guess.'

Ignoring his unveiled insult, I lie. 'Pleasure... um...' I pause. 'I don't know your name,' I realise.

'We Narration don't have names as such. You may simply call me Narration.'

Now we're on first-name terms, kind of, it feels a good time to broach the subject of his invisible companions. 'Are you all Narrations?' I tread lightly.

'Narration,' he corrects. 'I am a Narration, and am one of many Narration. And this lot,' – he whips his cane backwards – 'are just hitchhikers I've picked up over the years. What?' His eyes flash right. 'You are just hitchhikers... Then what?... Deputy Narration! How dare you! I'll beat you for even considering it.' With a woeful sigh his eyes roll to the left. 'Okay... Okay... *Okay*... What about helpers?... Okay!... Assistants?... Okay... Okay! You're *deputies*.' The voice in his left ear seems to hold some sway over him.

'What did you say their names were?'

'Arik-boke is the stocky fellow leaning against the wall.' He swings his cane to the dark wood panelling to my right, still with eyes fixed on me, still with fingers in motion. An expectant silence falls – what's he waiting for? The Narration indicates his absent colleague a second time.

'Hello, Arik?' I venture.

This appeases him. 'Well, it's Arik-boke, but he doesn't mind. Kazuo you've already met, and the little beauty to my left who seems to have taken a shine to you is Lady Jane Atherton.'

'Hello,' I greet again, trying not to look any-where in particular.

'Aww, I think we've embarrassed him – he can't even look at you. No idea when they turned up, but I took them in. Watching humans for 60,000 years can get lonely.'

'Did you say 60,000?'

'Indeed,' he answers in a weary tone. 'I've narrated kings' cousins, queens' concubines, Kubla Khan's curtain hanger, the Grand Duchess Anastasia and enough evolving homo sapiens to fill a thousand caves. All of them dispensing the same boring revelations; *must mate, is that it, time to die,* well the ones that could manage conceptual thought anyway. You humans are all pretty much the same in the end. Your lives are just a blink of the eye, but to you they're everything.'

The slightly crazy persona is starting to make sense. Miracle he's not completely insane. The benefit of make-believe companions, I guess. I can't be bothered bursting his coping bubble. 'I guess that's how you know so many forms of sword fighting?'

'Eight,' he says, lifting his cane to eye level. 'I've watched eight swordsmen from all over the world master their craft, man and boy, and as my wards have learnt, so have I. And not just swordsmanship. In my years I've learnt how to cross-stitch, throat sing, trap and kill white mammoth, seduce nuns, dance the fertility dance of the Myna people, bite the head off a variety of snakes and spot a man of means from fifty yards. I've studied every religion, language, culture and society in the history of man and, of course, I am an expert in raising children. I've watched 956 young ones raised. Although, the first loves are my favourite.' He allows himself the slightest of reminiscing smiles. It sits weirdly on his face. 'There's nothing like love that you're desperate not to lose.

The sweetest love is that which you cling to with just the tips of your fingers as it spins faster and faster. Always knowing one day you'll have to let go or be thrown to the floor.' The Narration's eyes drift away, and for the first time his fingers pause. 'I've seen love and loss so many times. First cuts into the fresh flesh always scar the deepest.'

I try to re-engage him. 'That's quite a life.'

A glint of sadness shoots across his eyes. 'Oh no, I've viewed some amazing lives, but mine has been spent sitting in that chair watching. It is my allotted place to watch lives fulfilled and lost, never to have my own. Being a Narration is my purpose.'

It's a duty that seems to weigh heavy. I change the subject. 'What's your accent? I recognise it but can't place it.'

Even in his melancholy he can't help but laugh. His fingers launch back into action. 'It's your accent! I've been alongside you every step of the way for twenty-six years, so inevitably I've picked up the same intonations and pronunciations. If you're interested, it's ninteen per cent of your mother's well-tutored, school-book Suffolk accent, fourteen per cent of your father's polite society broken nouveau Essex accent, three per cent grandparents, eight per cent of those insufferable posh kids from your first school, nine per cent your fun friends, seventeen per cent first love – told you it cuts deep – two per cent second love, eight per cent office politics, twelve per cent television, three per cent films, two per cent grunge phase, one per cent Britpop phase, one per cent of that Dickens thing you all seem to have and one per cent broken Austrian from that summer you wanted to be the Terminator.'

That was a good summer. I rub my face and forehead. 'That's very precise.'

'It's the facts.'

'Do you always pick up accents?'

'Every time; it's infuriating. If you could only comprehend the forms of communication I've mastered then you'd understand what a damned laboursome speech impediment of an inflection your accent is – dull and colourless as a wet pencil. I've spoken some of the finest and purest languages in history, from every pitch of Neolithic man's grunts to the poetry of the great Greek scribes. So the way your bland dialect sticks to my lips like the leftovers of a greasy chicken banquet is very upsetting.' His stare glazes a little. He really hates his (my) accent.

With a dismissive flick of his wrist the fire bursts back into life and Hattie Harris returns, even clearer than before. She's packing up to go home, still talking to Brenda on the phone.

'How does it work?' I ask.

'No *how*, just *is*.'

I study the image. 'You've watched my entire life, through this fireplace?'

'It's my portal to your world. Well, to you.'

'If you've been watching me, why are we looking at Hattie?'

The Narration considers. 'Look closer. We're not watching your colleague, but your empty desk. Stare at the chair.'

I do. 'So?'

'Do you see that faint line of a body?'

He's right, there's a misty aura sitting there. 'Yes, I see it. Is that my...' the words stick to my tongue '...ghost?'

His head rocks from side to side. 'Apart from your earthly remains that lie in the morgue, that is all that's left of you. Ghosts are how you humans describe the phenomenon.'

I watch Hattie. 'Can anyone see me?'

'Maybe, out the corner of an eye or in a fleeting glimpse, but when they look back you'll be gone. It's only because we're focused on you that we can see it now.'

My brow furrows. 'But I thought ghosts were souls trapped on Earth, not able to move on? I've moved on, so why do I still have a ghost?'

My Narration lets out an angry cry. 'Not that damned Swayze film again!'

'*Ghost*? I haven't watched it that many times.'

'Not many...! Twenty-seven fucking times! I've had to chronicle each one. That "All my love" song still makes Arik-boke nauseous. And that's saying a lot considering we sat through your encounter with Helen Truman.' He shudders. 'What a terrorising sexual happenstance that was. How did you describe it, Arikboke?' My Narration's mood seems to be improving at my expense as he keenly listens to the empty space behind. 'That's it,' he bellows as a wheezing laugh escapes his nostrils, 'like a drunk zookeeper trying to tickle an angry warthog through a letterbox.'

I can't in all honesty disagree, so I try a diversion. 'You were going to tell me about my ghost.'

He looks distracted. 'What? Oh yes, your ghost. Sorry, having trouble getting Helen out of my mind. Thunder and lightning, what were you thinking?' He directs a wry smile left. 'Of course we all know what you were thinking. She had loose clothes and even looser morals and you were young, stupid and horny. You are such a horny little bastard—'

'*Anyway*,' I interrupt.

'What?'

'My ghost!'

'Your ghost, yes your ghost,' he considers, 'in fact every ghost is nothing more than a shadow of the mundane existence you humans follow. Entire lives based on routine and repetition, embedding traits like deep scars into your spirits. So deep that when you die your ghost has no choice but to continue walking the same well-worn path. That's why we see yours, sitting at your desk, trapped in the same mundane chores that filled your working life. It will do this for years until it finally fades away. It won't feel pain when it goes, it's not conscious, or even alive, simply a reminder that you were once there.'

One of the unseen contingent chips in. 'Yes, it was quite poetic, wasn't it,' the Narration congratulations himself.

I watch my ghost. He's slumped over the keyboard staring vacantly at the screen. Condemned to mind-numbing communications until he fades away, poor bastard. Considering this, and on some level mirroring him, I slump forward and stare vacantly at my Narration's typewriter sitting on the little desk.

He glances at it, too. 'Beautiful, isn't it. Turn the feed bar, I've something to show you.' The handle is stubborn and makes that familiar typewriter rasping sound as it turns. On the third revolution a page pokes out. The handle gradually loosens and more and more of the page appears until, with a tug, I free it from the typewriter's grip. Print covers the entire sheet. 'I know you dislike reading aloud, so feel free to read to yourself if it makes you feel more comfortable.'

Of course he knows! The first thing that jumps from the page is my name, repeated over, and over, and over again.

Milton leans across to press the bell but the second young mother beats him to it. Milton steps off the bus and seems to have lost his work pass again. Before crossing the road Milton spots the young children looking down at a deceased frog in the road. They converse.

The page blurs. 'Is this my death?'
'It is,' my Narration simply replies.
'You watched all of this?'
'I did.'
Tentatively, I read on.

Milton: I think you two should stand on the pavement, don't you?

   Milton: Eek! Is that a dead frog?

   Girl: Yes.

   Girl: Fog's eye's out.

   Milton: So it is, that's pretty horrific.

   Milton: Maybe you should go back to your mums.

Milton ushers them back to their mothers. Milton turns back to cross the road and looks right. A blue hatchback driven by a man in his sixties comes from Milton's left and hits him. Milton is thrown 4.7 metres and lands in the middle of the road.

   Damage report: right leg broken, three broken ribs, heart punctured, internal bleed, he is conscious.

Milton is in a huge amount of pain. Milton stops breathing. Milton passes through the fire into the Afterlife. Milton's earthly body dies, but his Afterlife body survives. I drag Milton's body from the fireplace and lay him on the healing stone.

I consider the smear of blood leading from the fireplace to the stone table. 'Did I come through the fireplace? Is that the fire you were talking about?'

'You did. At the moment you took your last gasp, the mortal world and the Afterlife crossed, and your body, flesh, blood and bone all existed simultaneously in both dimensions. Then, your earthly body dies but your Afterlife body lives on; you live on. There's more.' He points at the sheet.

Vitals Report: Broken bones healing. Breathing is improving, indicating his lungs are mending. I will have to remove the heart, no need for it now, but I will need to find some way of boosting his life force.

I glance at the mutilated heart. 'That's mine?'

'It is.'

I rub my eyes. They're starting to suffer in the dim light. 'But how...?' I just about ask.

He taps his chest. 'See for yourself.'

Taking his lead, I gently tap my chest. It echoes wooden and hollow. Levering myself out of the small chair, I lift my T-shirt to reveal... a door, a little wooden door. It's circular and has been painted green and red, like a gypsy caravan. 'What is that?'

'Open it.'

I take hold of the wooden handle and open up my chest. Arching my neck forward, I'm suddenly struck by vertigo tremors. Clutching the desk, I just about steady myself. Collecting composure, I peer forward again and, breathing deeply, look inside. I stare in disbelief. 'Is that my hamster?'

Here I am, in the Afterlife with my pet hamster Penfold Fingerstick, and his little yellow exercise wheel stuck in my chest. 'Get him out of there!' I make a grab for him.

'No,' snaps my Narration. 'That little critter may be all that's keeping you alive. Your body is feeding off his life force and,' he adds with a proud grin, 'that little wheel is pumping blood round your newly emptied chest.'

'So... I'll die if he's not in there?' I ask uncertainly.

'You're already dead,' he blurts.

'Then what?' I frown.

'No idea.' He shrugs. 'This is new ground for all of us.'

'Fuck me,' I gape, still fighting the urge to remove the fluffy enema. I stagger round the edge of the desk. I breathe deeply, then look again. This time I notice the fleshy void round the plastic wheel – it's too much. The desk disappears from under my hand. I'm falling. Jolted by the shock, my senses snap back just in time to feel my Narration's little body break my fall. 'Thanks,' I wheeze to the small man lying under my torso.

His small knee connects sharply with my ribs. 'Get off me, you oaf!'

I leap up at the bee sting pain. 'Okay, okay,' I say. 'That hurt!'

'It would have hurt a lot more if I'd let you crack your head open on the floor,' he gripes, getting to his feet and dusting down his robes, 'and close that door before you ruin my work.'

Propping myself against the desk, I carefully close the door and leave Penfold Fingerstick to his running. My Narration taps the desk with his cane. 'Read on...' he prompts, dropping my shirt. I take a few more deep breaths, then reach for the pages.

I've managed to find a suitable replacement for Milton's heart in his Passover room. The replacement should give him more than enough strength to make the journey. It seems that Milton's changing dream is about butterflies. He is continuously muttering about his beautiful wings.

My focus rolls back up the words to *Passover room*. 'Is this my Passover room?' I ask.

He fixes me with a stern glance. 'No, this is the residence of a Narration. You came here from your Passover room.'

I can't hide my confusion. 'I came from my bedroom.'

'No, you came from your Passover room. I should know; I designed it.'

Further confusion. 'That wasn't my bedroom?'

'Nope, that was Purgatory.'

'Purgatory!' I glimpse back. 'As in the place between Heaven and Earth?'

'The same.'

'But it looked so real. Where did all the stuff come from?'

'Your real bedroom, of course. I sent a removal team in the moment you died. They're a hell of an outfit.' My Narration gives the grunt of a satisfied customer. 'Pride themselves on being rapid and meticulous. They memorised every inch of your bedroom and rebuilt it in Purgatory. Tests prove this method of transition is thirty-eight per cent more effective for a calm and incident-free passage into the Afterlife.' He directs me back to the pages I hold with a subtle nod. 'Continue.'

My last act as Milton Pitt's Narration was to take him back through the portal to his Passover room and lay him down. Milton's Passover room has been designed to perfectly match his current bedroom in Cowley, Oxford. Every detail is exactly the same, with the exception of Penfold Fingerstick who is, of course, in his chest. Milton's exit point will be his Passover room door. This will take him to the next place. My exit point will be hidden in the chimney and out of sight so Milton will have no choice on waking but to leave via what he thinks is the bedroom door.

He walks alongside a set of bloody footprints I hadn't noticed previously entering the fireplace.

'These are the steps that screwed me,' he says, tapping each one with his cane. 'After I fixed you, you're welcome by the way...'

'Um, thanks,' I venture.

'Don't mention it. I must have walked through the pool and trampled blood all over his Passover room.'

Leaning forward, I get a better view of the footprints. Sure enough, the thick bloody footprints that I followed from the far side of the room start here. 'The fire is a doorway to my Passover room as well?'

'Clearly,' he answers, with a disgruntled look towards me as if it couldn't be more obvious. 'You didn't think I dragged you back through that maze, did you?'

'I didn't really consider it.'

He doesn't reply. Instead, his eyes wander to somewhere aside from his three colleagues. It's the first time he's done that, and leaves an awkward silence between us.

Losing my discipline for a moment, my eyes linger too long on the movements of his fingers. They're so odd.

'What are you looking at?' His eyes are back on me. 'Why have you got that *they're so odd* look slapped all over your face?' he demands.

Goddamn, his mood is volatile. Is he reading my expression? Panicked, I cease all movement in my face. He's glaring at me. Quick, say something. 'Why are you doing that?'

'Doing what?' he snaps.

Shit. 'Um... well... moving your hands like that?'

'Like what?' His eyes dart left. 'What's he talking about?... No I'm not.' My Narration looks down at his dancing hands. 'What in God's name are they doing?' Baffled, he lifts his fingers to eye level and scrutinises them as if they belong to someone else. 'They're typing? Why are they typing?' He stares some more. 'I can't stop them.' There's desperation in his voice. Switching his focus, he catches me gaping. He grasps his cane tight and thrusts both hands behind his back. To create a natural break in the uncomfortable moment, I sit back down in the tiny seat behind the desk.

Dragging the cane behind him like a matador's cape, he turns to the wall of treasures. I watch, rocking onto the back legs of the chair, easy on such a small piece of furniture. Trying his hardest not to look back or move his fingers, he inspects the wall.

'Have you been collecting it all your life?' I try to calm his angst.

He glimpses me from the corner of his eye. 'I have. This represents thousands of years of cherished possessions of now past humanity. Mostly crap, but I make sure I keep at least one special item from each ward. Small reminders of my past.'

I crane my neck to follow him. 'If you've taken a keepsake from every human you've ever watched, why haven't you taken—' I don't finish. 'My Cuba book! But why take that? You have some of the most spectacular treasures I've ever seen and all you take from me is a tatty book?'

'It's not about the book.' His voice softens almost to the point where I can't hear it. 'It's about you. The person it made you. The adventure in those pages brought you to life. That's what we want to remember.'

I smile; even with all that anger I think he cares for me in his own way. 'It's definitely yours. I won't need it where I'm going.' I glance at his shaking hands clamped behind his back. 'You don't have to stop moving your fingers on my account.'

'I'm a 60,000-year-old being of the Divine. I think I can control a grade three repetitive stress disorder with obsessive compulsive tendencies.' Sliding his hands to his side, he turns to face me. 'See, I'm fine.'

'Good.' We both know he's far from fine.

'I'm fine,' he repeats, giving one of his people an exasperated look.

I re-read the last couple of lines of the last page of my life.

Milton's exit point will be his Passover room door. This will take him to the next place. My entry point will be hidden up the chimney and out of sight so Milton will have no choice on waking but to leave via the bedroom door.

'Why didn't you come back through the fireplace?' I ask.

'That's not how it works. It's a one-way deal, and only one time. I took you through the fireplace, and then the link was broken.'

I think back. 'That's why the footprints led up the chimney.'

'Yes, now forget the chimney!' he snaps.

'Okay,' I reply. Silence again; with slow throaty breaths that blow the matted hair hanging over his face; he sinks into another bout of self-pity. I take the opportunity to slip these pages into my pocket along with the others I grabbed earlier. Rocking back and forth on the rear legs of the little leather chair; another question comes to me. 'Where does my bedroom door lead?'

He scoffs a laugh. 'That's for you to discover.' The question seems to have shaken him from his stupor. 'But first, could you help me with something?'

This catches me off guard. I have no idea how I can help him. 'Um, yeah, sure, no problem.'

'Before we move on, the pages have to go into the fire. But my height doesn't make it so easy and this lot detest manual labour.'

Plus the fact that they're figments of his lonely imagination, but I keep that to myself.

'Yes, of course,' I say without hesitation. I suddenly feel a little guilty for stealing a few pages, but I don't say anything. 'Why are you so small?' I ask without properly thinking about the question.

His eyes blaze. 'I am a Narration,' he sneers, 'one of the oldest and holiest races in existence,' –

spittle flies from his lips – 'I am not small. You are an oversized and poorly balanced ape.' He strikes the bottom of my chair with his cane, sending me tumbling backwards. My head strikes the floor with a sharp crack.

Damn, that hurts. Note to self: don't comment on a Narration's height. I pick myself up. 'Sorry,' I murmur and climb onto the desk to scoop up a handful of pages.

He takes them from me. 'Thank you, and apologies if I hurt you. We Narration are proud folk. It is my duty to defend our honour. I can't help myself.'

'It's okay. I'm dead anyway, so what's a little more pain?'

He smiles. 'That's a good attitude.' He unceremoniously flings the pages into the fire. They incinerate as if soaked in paraffin. I can't smell anything flammable – what caused that? The second load burns just as vigorously and this time a white spiral of smoke rises from the flames. The third pile thickens the spiral further. It's hypnotic.

'So,' I venture, 'why are we burning all this?'

He gives me a quizzical glance. 'Because that's what we Narration do.' He hurls another three years of my life on to the fire.

'Why?' I ask. I'd have liked to read more. It'd be like taking a very detailed walk down memory lane.

'That is the way it has always been,' he answers. 'We chronicle a life, then pass it through the flames.'

I watch the pages in the fire. 'But they're just burning.'

'Burning, but not just burning,' he says.

I look again. No, they're just burning. Although there is something odd about the way the smoke is moving. It isn't going up; it's spiralling round and round, getting thicker.

'That is the knowledge of your life collecting.'

As more and more pages disappear, the smoke swells until it spills out of the fireplace. But still doesn't rise.

My Narration scoops the last pages off the desk and gently places them in the fire. With a click of his fingers the entire swirl of smoke is sucked up the chimney, disappearing with a roar. Then, with a wave of his hand, the fire dies down to nothing more than a smoulder. 'You need to leave,' he tells me, then turns and shuffles to the stone table.

Placing both hands flat on the cold hard surface, he begins to mutter. I can barely hear, and what I do hear I can't understand. It doesn't look like he's going to elaborate.

Where am I meant to go? Raising a tentative finger, I try to get his attention. 'Do I leave through the tunnel?'

Nothing. He couldn't peel his eyes from me a moment ago, now he couldn't be less interested.

A dull tremor vibrates up my leg. 'What was that?'

Again, nothing.

I raise my voice. 'Can you hear me?... How do I leave?'

His concentration breaks. 'Stand by the wall,' he snaps and continues his mysterious chant. Suddenly, I feel like I'm trespassing again.

Wish he'd make up his mind. Probably best to do what he says. I back up until I feel the varnished wood panelling against my shoulder-blades. From here I can see the entire room. But it's not as it was. With each word from his mouth the huge piles of relics and trophies vibrate and sway as if caught in the warning tremble of an earthquake. I press my fingers against the wall. There's a definite vibration travelling through the room. A distant rumble becoming louder as the treasures start to fall.

My Narration's chanting raises to a bellowing cry. He looks in pain. Sweat pours from his brow and his entire body shakes. A sharp piercing crack echoes round the room, stunning me. The stone table lies broken.

He beckons to me and his make-believe entourage. 'Come, all of you, come here.' I manage several quick steps before a tremor unbalances me. I stumble towards the... it's gone! The table has completely disappeared. A massive shockwave knocks me from my feet. Tumbling forward, I see it. A huge hole has opened and consumed the table. It's too late... I can't stop... I'm falling head first into the gaping void... disappearing into the black below. A small hand grasps my ankle. Everything blurs as I swing up and across the floor to safety. Relative safety anyway. Sliding to a messy halt, I seem to be back in the pool of blood.

'You saved me,' I gasp.

'Unbalanced ape,' I hear him grumble. 'Get up, there's no time.' Nothing is still. The floors, walls, the ceiling and the piles of treasures, all shaking violently. 'Move!' shouts my Narration, shoving me out of the way of a massive marble statue as it slides across the floor and disappears into the hole. 'The hole is creating a vacuum. Out! Now!'

A large section of the antique wall suddenly breaks away and crumbles into the hole. My Narration points towards the gap it leaves. 'There, follow Kazuo. *Go!*' he yells. Leaping and ducking we launch ourselves into the opening.

Towers crash down. It feels like I mustn't stop for a second. I drop to the floor as a chair flies over my head, I dive over a crouching taxidermied tiger and spin to avoid a tribal spear hurtling point-first through the mayhem. Unlike me, my Narration moves gracefully through the chaos, bounding from object to object, riding the wave of treasures. Unless I move faster I'm going to lose him. Trying to imitate him, I spring on to a chaise longue and run its length as it whisks by. Leaping again, I clear a colossal vase and hit the floor just in time to roll under a horse-drawn carriage.

'I can see the exit staircase,' he calls back to me. It's all the encouragement I need to hurdle a spinning cannon then drop my shoulder into the last line of relics. I reach the bottom step of the staircase and grasp the railing. My Narration is already at the top, holding open the small door to my bedroom chimney. 'Hurry!' he calls over the roar of the wind. But the vortex is dragging me back. With my muscles straining, I cling to the staircase, edging forward like a high-altitude climber. Using the railing as a ladder, I finally reach him. Anchoring himself to the circular brass handle on the door, my Narration throws out his hand. I almost miss, his hand is so small, but stretching, he hauls me up. The pull on my body is so strong I lift into the air – but inch by inch I'm able to lock my legs through the doorway and, with his help, slide back into the confined space of my chimney. Gasping for breath, I look back into the now empty room. But there's no time. Anchoring myself, I offer my hand. 'I'll pull you in.'

He smiles strangely, no panic or worry clouding his eyes. 'That's not our way,' he tells me over the howl of the swirling wind. 'You three go. I'll follow,' he instructs the empty space at the bottom of the staircase.

I stare past him at the gaping hole. 'Where does it go?'

'That's the gateway to my next world; all my belongings have already travelled there, just me left to go.'

'Hey!' I notice his free hand isn't moving. 'You're cured.'

He holds it up to his face and rhythmically rolls his fingers a couple of times. 'Of course I am. I'm a Narration. Goodbye, Milton Pitt. I've enjoyed watching you.'

With that, the little Narration exhales like one who is at peace and lets go of the handle. His body goes limp as he is whisked into the room. Then, like a spider down a drain, my Narration disappears to narrate another life.

The second he disappears the wind in the room reverses, blowing in my face rather than drawing me towards the hole. This unexpected gust catches the back of the little door and slams it shut, encasing me in the chimney. I push against it but it's shut tight. So that's it; I guess I have no choice. Losing my grip, I slide down the chimney and tumble back into my room.

VII

3 hours 4 minutes after

Back in familiar surroundings, these past few hours seem unreal. I scan the room as I did when I woke this morning, and as they did this morning, my eyes come to rest on my hamster cage. '*Penfold.*' I run my hand up my chest and feel the door, still there, little wooden handle and all. That's certainly real, and so are the now dry bloody footprints. I can't believe I didn't notice that they don't arrive from the chimney – only leave. I follow the footprints to their starting point. Sure enough, they materialise from thin air, just start walking in the middle of my room. Or whatever this room is. The Narration was telling the truth – the portal opens up and through he walks, dragging me behind him. This is more than enough reassurance. I'm not mad – just dead.

I should draw my curtains before I go. Through the crack I see the light outside is unusually crisp and white. If this is Purgatory, what's out there? I pull the curtains apart. With a startled gasp I stumble backwards into my desk and tumble to the floor.

I crawl back to the window. Breathing deeply, I place my finger-tips – the ones I still have – onto the windowsill and raise my eyes. The crumbling brick wall, car-lined road and mirror-image terraced houses have been replaced by... the extraordinary. On the other side of the dirty glass a single clear blue sky stretches in all directions. And I mean, all directions. My eyes free-fall downwards until they land on the top of thick porcelain clouds shining in a way I've only experienced from a plane. Minutes pass as I stare at this private piece of sky that has become my front garden. This definitely isn't my bedroom. A sail-shaped cloud catches a gust of wind, tearing a hole in the endless silken cover. Green shapes show themselves. That's Europe. My God! Purgatory really does float somewhere between Earth and the Heavens. How has it never been discovered? I even see England before it disappears behind a rolling boulder of clouds following closely in the sail's wake.

I sigh to compose myself, then stand. It's time to confront my future in the Afterlife. Peering into the corridor, I see the same flaky green paint and worn-out floorboards. But when I step out, nothing is the same. No familiar wooden staircase, landing window or airing cupboard. Instead, there's endless corridor in both directions. Which way? They really should make this more clear; death is confusing enough without poor directions. I turn back to my room. If I stay here much longer I'll chicken out altogether.

Chickening out just for a minute, I ponder a change of clothes. Comfort is probably key in Purgatory. I go for some jeans, my favourite white chequered shirt and worn-in leather boots. I wonder if it'll be cold. I'll risk it; I look good in this shirt.

Something drops onto the floor as I change. It's the pages I stuffed in my pocket. I ended up taking quite a few. Flicking backwards through the pages it seems like I've got everything from the moment I woke this morning to the moment my Narration signed off. Sitting on the edge of my blood-stained bed, I scan through the little pages until something catches my eye.

7.43am: Milton's glimpse begins.

'What's my glimpse?' I say to myself.

Milton: Penfold?
    Milton: Is that you?
    Milton: You sneaky little bastard. How did you get out of your cage?
    Milton's eyes look to the sound, his eyes narrow in the sunlight. A naked, bald-headed woman with a birthmark on her lower back appears at the end of the bed.

I forgot all about that. It really happened? I really saw her – shit, I need to ask my Narration about her. Too late now. Mournfully, I glance back at the chimney. Why didn't I ask him about the woman?

Milton: Hello?

Milton: Hello?

The woman doesn't react to Milton's greeting. Milton moves forward and reaches out to touch her. The radio plays music.

Milton: You hear it.

The woman rapidly turns to face Milton. They stare at each other. Milton gasps, stumbles backwards and closes his eyes. Milton opens his eyes. The woman is gone. 7.45am: Milton's glimpse ends. Milton looks at the clock radio and around the room in a confused state.

How was that real? Who was she? Why was she here? I feel a twinge of regret mixed with a strange craving to know more. I read the words again. 'Who are you?' I mumble to myself, stuffing the pages into my pocket. My attention floats to my phone. Should I call someone... to say bye? Mum and Dad, maybe. Or I could tell work I won't be in. Or cancel the TV licence. Nah, that's the benefit of death – someone sorts that out for you. But I can't pass up the chance to speak to my parents one last time. Should I tell them I'm dead? Leaning forward, I pick up the receiver. There's no dial tone. It's dead. Figures. I didn't think too much about my family until now. Suddenly, the reality of losing them feels like a huge weight round my neck and I thud back down to the bed, unravelling to lie flat with my arms stretched out. I don't move for several minutes.

Okay, no more chickening out. Backward-rolling to my feet, I return to the corridor, take a breath, close my eyes and spin on my heels. It appears I'll be going right. 'Goodbye, bedroom,' I bid as I begin to walk. Ten paces on, the wooden floor and flaky paint give way to large, grey stone slabs. I guess they had no reason to decorate the corridor any further than this. Quickly my landing turns into a hallway better suited to a medieval castle. Cautiously, I place my weight on the uneven stones, worn as though they've been here for centuries. This corridor needs some love and attention. I kind of expected more from the Afterlife.

I consider the space. 'The Afterlife, hey?' I cast my mind back to R.E. lessons. 'They do say a place always sounds better in the brochure.' These words echo into the dark space. Picking up pace, I feel like I'm entering an ancient crypt.

A creeping excitement grips me as I move further along the constricted space. What will I find? It feels wrong to commit so resolutely to a direction with no idea where it leads, especially when it's down an increasingly dark tunnel lit only by candles set into the wall. But my Narration's instructions make as much sense as anything else, so I forge on, impatient to see where it leads.

Three hours later I've somewhat lost my enthusiasm. I stop to rest. Probably should have brought a drink or snack. Actually, now that I think about it, I'm not hungry or thirsty – strange. Maybe it's a death thing. I wonder how long I can go without food. Sliding to the floor, I stretch my legs across the width of the corridor. What now? How long do I keep walking? Where am I meant to go? A shiver of uncertainty runs through me.

Then a faint sound reaches my ears. Voices? Sounds like they're a long way away, but it's enough to stir my excitement. I jump to my feet and run to the next corner. The voices grow louder. Three corners later the voices are clear and accompanied by a chorus of shuffling feet, lots of feet. Adrenaline pumps as the hum of hundreds gets closer. One voice rises above the others, bouncing off the hard walls and echoing around me. It's giving instructions of some kind. I can't hear exactly, but I know a regimented delivery of orders when I hear it.

I glance round every corner before turning, like coppers sweeping a criminal's house. Intrigued as I am by the voices, I don't want to come face-to-face with the fuckers without getting a look first. I sidle up to the next corner. I'm close. I can hear the voice clearly now. It has a strange crackle like it's coming from an old speaker.

'This is your bus conductor speaking. You are waiting in line for the 3.25 to Exeter, which will

*be arriving in seven minutes, but only if you're
good! Tickets may be purchased on the bus and
will be unexpectedly expensive.'*

A bus conductor? What's going on? Maybe
they've confused Heaven with Devon. Following
the sound, I poke my head round the next corner.
Nothing. Damn, these corridors are deceptive. Next
corner, same process, same outcome. Nothing, apart
from the voice.

*'In accordance with our governmental legislators,
please refrain from eating hot food, smoking,
listening to music, making loud noises, listening
to loud noises, making eye contact, standing in
front of any lines anywhere, wearing hats or
biting people. Please consider the feelings of all
of your fellow travellers and have a nice day.
Oh, and don't forget your seat belt.'*

I see them! About twenty paces away a larger
corridor crosses mine and it's full of people. I
approach tentatively. The larger corridor is well lit,
not by candles but by a powerful glow bouncing off
the reflective walls and ceiling. The tannoy has gone
dead, but I can hear people talking. 'Well, I do like
the West Country,' someone in the queue says.

'I don't want to go to Exeter,' protests another.

'Well, it makes sense to me. That's where Bert's
family live,' says a rather well-to-do woman.

'I thought I was queuing at the post office,' comes another unseen voice.

'Why the hell do we have to wear seat belts on a bus?' echoes another from even further down the corridor.

They can't know they're dead. I can't believe they bought that bus lie. I guess you believe what you need to. Reaching the entrance to the tunnel, I poke my head in. It's like the Tube at rush hour. They all have that oddly placid look of cattle waiting to go to slaughter, calmly shuffling along the corridor sharing the odd word with each other, totally happy in their bus delusion. Why don't they question it? Maybe they think they're dreaming.

I guess I should join them. Slowly, I edge into a small space next to an old-timer. A really old-timer. I wouldn't be surprised if she was pushing 100 when she passed. She's wearing a lavish pink and blue dressing gown with fancy gold trim and matching pyjamas underneath. There's an unmistakably damp musk surrounding her, not unlike the smell of a charity shop.

She acknowledges my presence. 'I'm confused.'

I wonder which of the many confusing situations in this confusing transitional place she's referring to. 'What about?'

She squints at me from beneath pencilled eyebrows. 'I got up in the night to go to the toilet and now I'm queuing for the bus. What happened? I didn't even need to pee – just thought I'd give it a try while I was awake. And I think I'm wearing my husband's slippers. Am I wearing large chequered slippers?'

I glance down. They're at least three sizes too big for her. 'Afraid so.'

She shakes both fists in frustration. 'Damn. Do they look silly?'

'No, they look good,' I lie.

She studies my insincere expression. 'I'm not so sure,' she says, then seems to forget all about it. 'My daughter is going to kill me. Third time this month I've wandered off in the middle of the night. Last time she found me at Southampton docks with an old Labrador I'd bought from a tramp named Sebastian – the dog, not the tramp,' she clarifies. 'I was trying to barter a passage to India with a bucket of fried chicken and my wedding ring. What a wonderful adventure that would have been. Sebastian made it on. I often wonder about the fantastical adventures he had aboard that ship.'

Seems it's still possible to be slightly mad in the Afterlife. Death is a strange enough place without stories like that. This old explorer is probably picturing Sebastian with a frayed bandana round his neck, living a buccaneering life at the feet of an eye-patched sea captain. More likely he ended up in an Argentinean sailor's stew. Oh well, probably best to leave her with her delusions. She is dead, after all.

She offers me a bony hand. 'I'm Queenie.'

'Milton.'

'Nice to meet you, Milton.'

I smile politely. 'You too.'

She glances uncertainly round the tunnel. 'I expect my daughter will be here soon to pick me up. Um, where are we?'

'I'm not sure.' Any other answer would involve telling her she's dead. I don't think she's ready for that.

'It's strange...' Queenie begins, but then pauses as if distracted. 'It's strange...' she tries and fails again. 'It's strange... what the hell is going on with that young man?' Queenie blurts out, pointing a withered, knotted finger at a self-important-looking hipster a few rows ahead.

'What?' I question.

'Why does he look like that?' she grumbles.

'Like what?' I indulge her.

'All busy and peculiar,' she tries to explain, 'like a poorly groomed pirate,' – Queenie tilts her head a little – 'or a well-groomed pony.'

I try to bring her back to her point. 'What were you saying? What's strange?'

'Um, yes it is strange...' Queenie considers, trying to divert her sunken eyes from the pony. 'I remember... having this awful pain in my chest, worse than I've ever felt before, and then suddenly it went away. That was just before I felt compelled to go to the toilet even though I didn't need to.'

'How odd,' I say.

'Yes it is odd, it really hurt, I actually thought my number was...' She pauses. 'I'm dead, aren't I?'

'Yes. We both are.' No point lying – she'll find out sooner or later anyway. 'In fact we're all dead.' I may have said that a bit too loudly. The black-haired woman in front spins round. 'We're all what?'

'He said we're dead,' chimes another a few rows forward. My voice is louder than I think. I've had this problem before, mostly when attending weddings and funerals. I'm always the one singing louder than anyone else.

'What was that?' comes from behind.

'We're dead. *We're all dead*,' cries the pony with a predictable amount of angst. The corridor erupts. Front and behind the waiting crowds fall like dominoes. Pandemonium breaks out with blood-burning agony, grown men and women weep like babies.

I feel a bit strange standing amongst this madness and disorder with a peaceful air. Gives me an odd sense of superiority – I'm not used to it. Glancing left, I notice one other person who isn't screaming, weeping or wailing. Queenie is standing next to me equally peacefully. 'Why aren't you writhing in anguish like the rest of them? You are dead, you know,' I remind her.

She doesn't turn to look at me. 'I know,' she says in a blasé tone.

I frown. 'Then shouldn't you be rolling around on the floor blubbering about the loved ones you'll never see again?'

'I have no interest in that.'

'Why not?'

'I'm old, lost my fear of death long ago. The way I see it – I wasn't really bothered about missing the first 200,000 years of human evolution, so why should I worry about missing the next 200,000 years, or even one year for that matter.'

Can't argue with a philosophy like that. 'You won't miss your loved ones?' I ask.

'Barely have any left. There's my daughter and her family, but they'll be all right without me. I dare say they'll even enjoy the inheritance. The rest are dead, so I'm more likely to catch up with loved ones here than there.'

'But what about your husband? You're wearing his slippers.'

She looks down at her wrinkled toe poking out of a hole. 'No, Albert's been gone three years now. I couldn't bear to throw his things away, not even these.'

'Do you think he's waiting for you?'

'I hope so.' Her face crumples to a smile. 'What about you?' she asks in return. 'I'm old. I've lived a long and fulfilling life, and by all accounts died in my home, in my bed, in my sleep, just a quick pain, no suffering and no misery, a pretty good way to go really. How old are you, twenty-nine? Thirty?'

'Twenty-six.'

'*Twenty-six*. You should be the one wailing about missed opportunities, plus you have a worrier's face.'

Did she just say I have a warrior's face? 'Um,

thank you, I've always thought I'd be a good warrior.'

'No, worrier.'

'Warrior?'

'Worrier, as in *to worry*, you have the face of a frightened squirrel trapped in a barrel.'

'That's not really a compliment, is it?' My God, first my Narration and now this old prawn. Do I really appear so gutless that people feel the need to comment on it? Maybe they have a point. 'I guess I was a worrier,' I admit after a moment's thought. 'I woke this morning worried that my life wasn't on schedule, my job wasn't as good as my friends', I had a huge mortgage that I couldn't afford, I didn't have a girlfriend, I hadn't experienced enough and my conversation was boring. But now all of those worries are over because I'm dead. I fixed all my troubles in just one day.'

Queenie glances down the corridor. 'Your conversation's still boring.'

The mayhem in the corridor has spiralled. The distressed masses are scratching at their eyes and faces, banging their heads against the floor and biting each other. 'Why?' One or two of them rather predictably scream. 'The gypsies, the gypsies, they'll steal all my children,' another quite unpredictably follows.

The entire corridor is a thunderous war zone, the howling is chilling. Judging by the depth of his misery, the pony must have been a big deal on Earth.

Lost in his wretchedness, he's smashing his forehead against the hard floor. I think I just saw a tooth fly past. His eyes are wild, almost animal; the loss of his earthly life has totally switched him.

Being incredibly English I do my best to ignore the extrovert horror all around. But if this mass hysteria continues I'll be queuing for ever. So, being incredibly un-English, I decide to skip the queue. I don't think I'll ask Queenie if she wants to come. She'd only hold me up – and she's weird. I leap over a weeping widow, trot over the pony and take off down the corridor.

Slowly but surely I build momentum. I'm making excellent progress. I only get stopped a couple of times by people angry at my queue-jumping, but I remind them they're dead and they fall out of the way.

What's that tingling round me? Weaving my way through the troubled multitudes, I'm more and more aware of a warm glow. Breathing deeply, I feel it in my lungs. It's great, cleansing my insides and fuelling me with an uplifting sense of confidence and peace. The wild and free glow runs through my veins warming my blood; it's intoxicating.

Anticipation bubbles in my chest as my jog turns into a run. Faster and faster. I'm not even noticing the crying masses any more, I feel way too good to be bothered with their misery. Come to think of it, I can't feel my legs. They're moving themselves – automatic pilot or something. I don't care. There's a warm wind embracing me, carrying me forward. I think it's changing the way I... um... think.

Someone in the queue screams with pain. 'Fuck you!' he shouts. Was that at me?

'Hey, no cuts!' demands another.

Another anguished cry. 'You bastard.' That was definitely at me. Why?

The floor's different. I look down. I see a boot stamping on someone's hand. A woman's hand. 'My hand!' she shrieks. I hear the brittle bones crack. That's my boot. That's my foot. I'm doing that. Should I be doing that? Looking down, I realise I'm stamping, kicking and bundling my way past anyone in my path. I'm sure I didn't think that trampling innocent people was okay before, did I? Whatever... I feel great now.

The tormented yells dissipate to a faint murmur as a musical note rings out from somewhere. What's that? Someone's singing. Who's singing? Am I singing? Oh my God, I'm singing. What's happening to me? With no need to take another breath, I sustain the musical note. It pulses from my lungs. It's imprisoned in the light all round me and has taken on a momentum of its own, bouncing round, leaving small pieces of me in every corner. It evolves, from a single note, to an entire hallowed choir. It's louder. I'm louder. I'm screaming, and the choir bellows back with a savage intensity. This light is furious. I close my eyes tightly, but it's just as bright on the inside. I'm going to burst.

Then peace. The eye of the storm. I stop running but still I sing my note. I open my eyes... and still I sing my note. I see the pearly gates... still I sing my note. I see Saint Peter sitting regally before the gates... still I sing my note. I'm smoking with the passionate flames of Heaven... still I sing my note.

Saint Peter stands up and clubs me in the neck... which really stings my throat. I can't breathe. I'm not singing. I think I'm going to pass out.

VIII

7 hours 39 minutes after

I wake in some kind of waiting room with a shooting pain in my neck. I wince. It all comes flashing back: the queue, the intoxicating light, that wonderful feeling and... *Saint Peter clubbing me*. This room is huge. Rows of metal-framed seats stretch endlessly in every direction, the sort you'd find in an airport waiting room all melded together into solid blocks of twenty or so. Tables are scattered around, all with well-thumbed pamphlets and magazines.

I seem to be wrapped in a big white sheet, fortunately covering my naked body. 'Where am I?' I mutter as my eyes regain focus.

'Purgatory's waiting room,' a soft voice replies.

I jerk my head towards the sound and the pain in my neck jerks back. A mousey-haired girl, probably in her twenties, is sitting a seat away from me wearing a very bookish dress. She's all green cardigans and brown shoes. Either she's a librarian or she's from the Blitz; I'm gonna go with librarian.

She's pretty. Well, pretty enough to stutter a breath if not take it away.

She spots the concussed bafflement slapped across my face. 'Sorry, I didn't mean to startle you.' Her manner instantly soothes me. She isn't smiling and I see sadness in her, but she has a kind face. I sense the kind of vulnerability that instantly warms you to a person. I feel comfortable with imperfections. People with their own concerns don't wait for you to stumble over your words or make a stupid statement; they're far too concerned with their own faults.

'Um, no you didn't. It's fine. Did you say Purgatory's waiting room?' I question, still not sure that I trust my ears.

Her hands tentatively drop into her lap and then by her sides. 'Yes, they sat you here after you passed out.'

I run my hand across my neck and Adam's apple. It's sore and my face is covered in dry blood. This could also be a reason for my stuttering breath.

With no further conversation forthcoming I absently turn my attention to the ever-multiplying rows of seats. I strain my eyes to see an end, but there is none, just a kind of indoor horizon as seats, people and waiting room blur to an indistinguishable distance. A dense disruptive rustling fills the air as thousands of people try to be silent. 'Why did Saint Peter club me?' I ask in lieu of other conversation.

'Who?' she replies.

'Saint Peter... he clubbed me,' I say with less conviction this time.

She directs my gaze a couple of rows back to a small iron-gated entrance where the corridor meets the waiting room. 'Do you mean Carl?'

'Who?'

'Carl.' She points to a stocky man with grey beard, bald head, white toga and a big gold club stuffed ominously into a velvet rope belt. No wonder I thought he was Saint Peter. I pick a piece of dry blood from my beard. 'Why did Carl club me? It hurt.'

She blushes a little. 'Well, you were standing there naked as the day you were born, screaming.'

I suspect I have the expression of a Saturday-night drunk as he tries to recall the previous evening's shenanigans in the cold sobriety of Sunday morning. 'I was?'

'I'm afraid so. Carl let you be for half a minute or so then cracked you in the neck. I think he meant to hit you over the head but missed. It looked painful. You stumbled around a bit, went blue and fell on your face. How are you now?'

I check my nose and the large cut on the side of my forehead. 'Okay... I think.'

She glances at the entrance again. 'And the corridor? Has it worn off?'

I stretch my eyes wide. 'I think so. I just feel a bit dazed now,' I say, trying to rub the stars from my eyes.

That was strange... why would Purgatory have a corridor that twists your mind? It turned me crazy.

'You skipped the queue, didn't you?'

'Um... well yes. How did you...?'

'Always happens to queue-jumpers.'

'What?'

'*The bliss bends* I think they call it. The corridor does more than just transport people. It alters their mood – from post-mortem blues to a warm and fulfilled peace. Gives you a shot of heavenly light directly into your core, but you're meant to enter the light slowly at the speed of the queue.' She now speaks with the confidence of someone who is energised by these kinds of random encounters. 'You skipped it so you got a week's worth of joy in a matter of minutes and burned the clothes from your body in the flames of ecstasy while you were at it. You overdosed.'

I don't like the sound of that. 'Does it leave any permanent damage?'

'No,' she half smiles, 'apart from euphoria and madness the effects are minimal.'

I fidget with the sheet. Slipping it over my shoulders, I'm able to make it look more like a dressing gown. Gingerly, I touch the side of my neck. 'He didn't have to club me,' I mutter, 'there's easier ways of quietening someone down even if they are out of it.'

'You'd think so, wouldn't you?' she agrees. 'But up here, over-the-top actions are normal, I'm afraid.

Nothing they like more in the Afterlife than a good knockout. Do it every opportunity they get. I've been knocked out or sedated more times than I can remember.'

I assume that's because of the number of times it's happened rather than concussion.

'Your naked singsong was the perfect excuse for their favourite pastime. Clubbing you was a bit brutal, even for them. Their usual method is potion or dust. As I said, they're all about the drama.'

Exhaling, I recline into my chair. 'Ah well, at least it's a story to tell um... someone. To be fair, it would have started my Afterlife on a real downer if my first heavenly realisation was that Saint Peter is a prick.'

The librarian smiles politely while digging around in one of her jacket pockets. 'Are these yours?' She holds up a wedge of crumpled papers. The pages I stole from my Narration.

I take them from her. 'Oh, yes, thanks.' These are hardy little bits of paper.

'What are they?' she asks, catching me off guard a little.

'They came from my Narration,' I answer without thinking. I'm still groggy.

'You met a Narration?'

'I guess so.'

'My God, a real-life Narration. Who'd have thought it.' Her eyes roll across the first few lines. 'Oh sorry, do you mind me reading this?' she asks, averting her eyes.

'Sure,' I say. 'Go ahead.'

'Thanks.' She takes a moment to read through the pages, then pauses and re-reads a particular page. 'Is this really your glimpse?'

'It's my last day alive,' I attempt to explain, aware that I may be missing something.

She sends me an enquiring look. 'You don't know?'

'Don't know what?' I try to keep up.

'This is your glimpse. Look, it says it here,' she holds up the page. '*7.43am: Milton's glimpse begins.*'

'Oh yeah, I remember seeing that. Is it good? Does that mean the bald woman was real?'

'Your glimpse is a vision of the Heaven that awaits you if you live an innocent life on Earth. The bald woman is not only real; she's your Heaven.'

I'm speechless.

'In the past, the Almighty had been very anti-glimpse,' she keenly continues. 'If a sign from God was needed, they didn't have faith to begin with, and didn't deserve the Heaven that awaited. But with the development and evolution of the human mind came self-understanding and learning, then followed scepticism and self-promotion. So the rules had to change a bit to help the good Lord keep the general public on the road to Heaven. He enjoys being aloof, but it was getting ridiculous, so the glimpse was rubber-stamped.'

'So, my bald woman,' I stutter out of my silence, 'was my glimpse?'

She gives a delicate nod. 'That's right.'

I take hold of the bridge of my nose. 'Which is God letting me know what's waiting for me in Heaven?'

'Right again,' she confirms with unwavering patience. 'Amazing, isn't it? Your personalised vision of the glory that awaits you in death.' She pauses, then seems to recall some additional information. 'Apparently, most glimpses don't even get noticed. I don't remember mine. The human mind is such an uncomplicated thing that when offered a glimpse of Heaven it's generally unable to understand what it's seeing. And then there are those people who are so deeply cynical or self-obsessed that they blindly refuse to see God's gift even when it's placed right in front of them. Visions are mostly shrugged off as déjà vu, a blissful dream... or a great orgasm,' she punctuates with an unexpectedly knowing glint in her eye.

I smirk, briefly wishing my glimpse of Heaven was during sex.

She flicks through the ruffled bunch of pages. 'Not many people are lucky enough to get a first-hand Narration account of their glimpse. You're honoured!'

'I guess so,' I say, failing to suppress a smug smile. God, I'm glad I stole those pages. 'You're very well-informed, by the way.'

'Thanks.' She smiles sweetly, and indicates the selection of poorly designed literature on the table.

'I read a pamphlet on it not too long ago; it obviously stuck with me.' She stares at me for a second more than is comfortable. 'Why do you think God sent you a bald, naked woman as your glimpse?'

'I have no idea. Aside from the obvious.' I grin and feel my face warming. 'I think it's worked though.' I compose myself. 'I can't stop thinking about her, and I really want to get to Heaven. Why do you think I saw her?'

Her thin eyebrows incline. 'I suppose it means she's your destiny in Heaven.'

'My destiny,' I slowly process.

'Yes, if you get there.' She delivers this news with the same sweetness.

'Did you say if I get there?' A murmur of anxiety creeps into my voice.

'Well, yes.'

'Might I not?'

'I don't know.' She scratches the inside of her wrist. 'The glimpse is the view of Heaven to push you to lead a just life, it's not a promise by any means. Have you lived a good life?'

'I reckon,' I say, not really sure what I'm being judged on.

'Well, I hope you get there.'

Conversation breaks until I sense her looking at my face. 'Do you want to wash yourself off?' she asks.

I touch the side of my face. 'Yeah, probably.'

'Toilets are over there.'

'Okay.' As I stand up, my white sheet falls. I grab it, but not in time. I flash her, hamster door, Little General and all.

My face and entire body blush. Quickly as possible I grasp the sheet to myself.

'Here, use this,' she chuckles, sliding a belt from the hoops of her dress. The belt secures the sheet quite nicely. Bending down, she picks something up. 'They got away from you again.' It's the pages.

I glance at the sheet. 'Can you hold onto them for me?' I don't have pockets. 'Are you going to be here long?'

'Sure. I've been here sixty years. I'll still be here when you get back,' she reassures.

'Won't be a second,' I whimper bashfully, and wander to the toilet door.

Wait. Did she just say she's been here for sixty years? How can she have been here that long? I'll ask when I come back. I don't even know her name. Need to get better at asking people's names when I meet them. With one hand on the toilet door, I awkwardly call back. 'Um... I'm Milton by the way.'

'I know,' she calls back, waving the small pieces of paper. 'I'm Annie. Annie Waits,' then mouths, 'nice to meet you.' I bundle my way awkwardly through the door and out of sight.

On the other side I'm faced by a long, enclosed staircase travelling all the way up to a small door at the very top. This isn't going to be easy in my makeshift toga. I put my foot on the first step of the completely white staircase. The steps are cold on my feet. Marble – how predictable.

I make good progress up the narrow stairs; all those embarrassing hours on the cross-trainer at the gym weren't in vain. Or maybe they were, as it wasn't poor health that killed me. *Damn it.* I've just paid a year's subscription – that's £400 I'm not going to get back.

The name suddenly sinks in. Annie Waits. *What's Annie Waiting for?* The little gravestone in the churchyard. Could it really be the same Annie Waits? She did say she's been in that waiting room for sixty years. But she looks my age. It can't be her. Can it? I want to turn round, walk back down the stairs and ask her. But I don't. As Annie said, she's been there for the last sixty years, a few more minutes won't matter. I'll get cleaned up then find out what she's waiting for.

As I approach the door at the top of the staircase, a leg-shakingly bad smell invades my nasal cavities. When I open the door, the stench hits me like an anvil to the face. Grasping hold of the banister, I back away. I'm going to be sick. It doubles me over, I take three or four shallow breaths and, only just suppressing the urge to gag, open the door again.

The bathroom looks a great deal like it smells. Like shit. It's a small and very compact multi-sensory assault. A moistened rag of a curtain divides a cubicle from the rest of the bathroom. A single sink that was probably white at one time now resembles a rash I once had, and a strange black fungus with red mushrooms grows in the urinals. In my many years of visiting backstreet bars I've never seen a bathroom that boasts this level of neglect. We're not talking weeks or months of abandonment, but years. Many, many years. The entire room is coated in a brown film, which seems to have infused everything it's touched in equal measure.

A man leaning against the filthy bathroom sideboard stares at me. How can he stand it in here? I think he's a freshen-up man. Before I can properly make him out I hear him softly singing a tune that I recognise, I think. What is it? His long, skinny, yellow-tinged face plays host to a multitude of sharp features, creating a stern facade. His odd tune doesn't falter as he stares at me with piercing white eyes from under a large purple velvet hat. Beneath his pointed chin is a crisp shirt collar and tightly fastened slimline neck tie contained by a long furry red coat. Tight yellow trousers and burgundy brogues finish the look. Even in these outlandish colours he's barely visible against the mould-stained corner of the bathroom. The long halogen light flickers off and on, giving the room and the freshen-up man a sinister feel. It's The Beatles, 'Rocky Raccoon' from *The White Album*, a classic. His version doesn't follow The Beatles' melodic upbeat tune; his is slow, quiet and more than a little eerie. The words roll off his tongue with the gravelly growl of an old jazz man telling the story of his life. It's a real performance – I hope he's not expecting a tip.

There's a tube coming out of the side of his mouth. We hold each other's gaze until my eyes can't help but follow it down to the floor into a metre-high shimmering orange glass shisha pipe, beautifully encased in an intricately crafted silver frame. Inside swirls a thick white smoke. The freshen-up man takes a long draw on the pipe, holds the smoke in his lungs for a second and then… nothing. Where did it go? I wait for him to give in and exhale. Maybe he's holding it in for dramatic effect. He even clears his throat with a satisfied grunt and continues singing. Still no smoke. It's disappeared – that can't be healthy.

He pauses. 'Freshen up?' he questions without a hint of emotion and not even bothering to direct my attention to the perfumes, colognes and fragrances littering the sideboard.

I automatically answer, 'No thanks.'

Cautiously, I walk to the sink. 'Just need to clean this blood off.'

The ominous scarlet pimp doesn't seem bothered. 'Suit yourself.' He goes back to singing.

Washing the blood from my face and hair, I consider reopening the conversation – a similar taste in music could be a good starting point. But he suddenly stops singing, and gags – maybe from the smell. I think he's going to be sick. His eyes have lost focus and he's retching. Here comes the puke! I slide away from the projectile zone as his gagging worsens, and then, like a volcano, he explodes, but not with vomit. I watch in shocked fascination as the freshen-up man, locked in constant convulsion, spews the thick white smoke. I splutter and cough as it fills the room. This is creepy.

'Are you okay?' I ask.

Nothing. Shaking my hands dry, I turn to make my escape.

I hear a voice from behind. 'Milton Pitt, is it?' he growls.

I freeze. He knows my name. How? I turn. He's standing there as if nothing has happened.

'How do you know my name?' I ask, one hand on the door handle.

He breaks into a smile. 'We're all about customer service here.' Slowly he spreads his arms wide and drops into the faintest of bows. 'Are you sure you won't freshen up?' His new tone warms the atmosphere in the room.

I release the door handle. 'Sure, why not,' I concede. He selects a beautiful jewel-encrusted bottle and sprays cologne onto my neck. It's unbelievable. I breathe in the intoxicating aroma. 'That's amazing.'

He looks a little like someone who has just given their pet a treat. 'You humans and your love of things that stimulate your senses. I do envy you.' He leans against the sideboard and picks up 'Rocky Raccoon' exactly where he left off. Someone's pretty full of his own self-importance, especially considering where he works. I listen for what feels like a polite amount of time. 'Are you a Beatles fan?'

He stops mid-chorus and gives me an odd look. 'Isn't everyone?'

'I guess.'

He doesn't release my stare. 'Is that all you've got to ask me?'

It feels like the answer should be obvious, but it isn't. I shake my head.

'Well, I have one question for you. Don't worry, just a bit of market research.' He grins with stained teeth.

Here we go, I think to myself.

He removes a reporter-style flip-pad and pen from one of his velvet pockets. 'How would you feel about moving your genitals?'

'What?' I recoil, instantly placing both hands on my privates.

'Your genitals. How would you like to move them? Nothing funny,' he disregards my concern, 'focus group research apparently suggests the human nose would be the most suitable place for reproductive organs. Would you like that?'

'No,' I answer without hesitation, 'they're fine where they are.'

This doesn't seem to make sense to him. 'You realise your erogenous zone is currently in your waste system, don't you? It's so unhygienic,' he bemoans. 'Like building a funhouse in the sewers, it makes no sense! Are you sure you don't want to mate with your nose? You could do it while kissing – it'd make the whole process a lot easier.'

'No!'

'But it's unsanitary to keep them there,' he persists.

'This bathroom is unsanitary; how can you stand to be in here? It stinks!'

'Figures,' he laughs. 'I spray you with cheap perfume a very cantankerous extended family member gave me last Christmas and you think it's happiness liquefied. Yet, here in this room you have the true smell of the rapture and all your uncomplicated nasal passages can tell your brain is that it smells bad. What a shame,' he says, breathing in the stench. 'So many dazzling levels.' He grins. 'Reminds me of The Fifth Day.'

'Anyway,' he sighs, looking me up and down, 'let's get rid of that smell for you.' He reaches into his jacket with purpose, but then stops. He looks stumped, annoyed even. 'How did you die?' he asks as if it's information he should already know.

'Um—'

'Actually, don't tell me,' he interrupts with a single beady eye fixed upon me. 'I'll know soon enough.' In a flash he's pulled a small bottle of perfume from inside his jacket and sprayed it directly into my eyes. I instantaneously smell, taste and feel the aroma. Everything goes black. My eyeballs are on fire. I feel faint. I'm falling. I hit the floor hard, losing all except the end of the freshen-up man's song.

IX

I wake with a start. What's going on? Did the freshen-up man sedate me? *That fucker*. Annie's right: these people really do like knocking you out. I'm going to start suing people if I ever get out of here. At least he didn't club me. 'Annie,' I recall belatedly. 'Where is she? Where am I?' I say out loud for some reason. Knew I shouldn't have gone to the bathroom.

Even before my focus returns, the musky air and dead sound suggests I'm not back in the waiting room. There's a strange movement to this small room. Reaching out, I find something rubbery down by my sides. I concentrate on my right hand and make out... a tyre. And a tyre on the other side. I'm in a wheelchair!

My vision expands – along with my confusion. Against the advice of all other senses, my eyes are telling me I'm in an endless room full of people. Why can't I hear them? Lots of them also seem to be in wheelchairs. Am I in hospital? One of them is staring straight at me. What does he want? Looks like a weirdo. Even through my haze I can tell he's wearing strange shit. I make out some yellow tassels, a bright purple velvet jacket buttoned to his waist and then unbuttoned to the knees, matching trousers, sandals, shoulder pads that look like flying carpets... and, are those war medals? He looks like the bastard offspring of Sergeant Pepper.

We watch each other. My eyes clear further and I lean forward. So does he. I raise my hand. So does he. I touch... glass. Is that me? It's a mirror – it's me. They're all me! Everyone in the room is me. I'm the Sergeant Pepper offspring! In the time I've been unconscious, some psycho (probably the freshen-up man) has removed my white sheet and dressed me. What the fuck is wrong with people in the Afterlife?

Looking into the never-ending prism this glass box creates, I inspect the multiple versions of me from every angle. Suddenly, within the reflections, a figure appears. Standing behind the wheelchair, standing behind this wheelchair! '*Oh shit!*' Stumbling from the chair, I hit the floor hard and pin myself against the mirrored wall.

'You all right, mate?' A young face leans over the back of the wheelchair.

'Who are you?' I demand.

'Tracey,' she replies. 'Why are you down there?'

'I'm not sure,' I say groggily.

'I think you should probably get back in the chair.

Can you manage?' Before moving I take a moment to eyeball her. She has cropped, greasy blonde hair – reminds me of a battered pigeon's dirty feathers. She's attempted to groom it into something resembling tidy, but it hasn't worked. The skin in transition between woman and girl is a conflict of flakes and sores. Another example of nature's purpose being one of pain and disfigurement. The rest of her is covered in an ill-fitting and grubby white shirt, clip-on tie and black trousers that probably fitted just before her last growth spurt. I don't think she poses a threat.

I relax, get to my feet and dust myself off. 'I'm fine.' I slump into the chair. 'It's been an unusual morning.' I consider my clothes. 'Did you dress me?'

'No,' she fires back. 'They told me you turned up pretty much naked. Had to dress you in something. Who knows why they dressed you in this abomination – must have raided the lost property.'

She talks with a youthful combination of misplaced confidence and disinterest. She's right about something: this outfit is an absolute nightmare.

I tug on the restrictive collar. 'Goddamn, this is humiliating.'

She smirks. 'Welcome to Purgatory.'

'Why am I in this wheelchair?'

'It's regulation, plus you were unconscious so options were limited. You can get out if you want.'

I'm enjoying the sit-down, plus my head isn't entirely together yet. 'No, I'm fine. Thanks.'

A moment's silence. 'Sorry, what did you say your name was?'

She spits on one hand, then the other. 'Tracey,' she returns, and vigorously smooths her eyebrows.

'I'm Milton. Nice to meet you, Tracey,' I say. 'Is this a lift?'

Tracey moves on to grooming her already slick fringe. 'What else?'

'Well... a little room.'

She grins to herself. 'Very intuitive. Yes, it's a lift. Didn't you wonder about the movement?'

I sense an upward motion. 'Now you mention it – yes. Where are the doors?' I scrutinise the walls.

'Right ahead of you.'

Straining my still throbbing eyes, I'm able to pick out the outline of the lift doors from the mirror wall. 'Oh yeah,' I say, 'well hidden, isn't it.'

Her reply is a disinterested grunt.

'It's a nice lift,' I continue, without any real goal in mind. 'Very clean.'

Tracey ignores this – her attention is on something under her fingernail.

I persist. 'The mirrors must've cost a bit.'

No reply again. I guess she's not a fan of lifts. Neither am I to be fair.

A glass display panel is inset above the door. Behind it floor numbers flip over like a ticker clock. 'Where are we going?'

'572.'

'So we're not going back to the waiting room, then?'

'No, 572,' she repeats.

'What's on floor 572?'

Tracey shrugs. 'Shit knows. I've never been there before.'

Nothing like customer service. 'Thanks for the update.' I think for a moment. 'Can we stop there on the way?'

'Where?' Tracey questions absently, leaning heavily on the back of the wheelchair while pretending to kiss into the mirror.

'The waiting room?'

'Obviously not.' She pauses from pouting to shoot me a dirty look. 'Why would you want to?'

'Oh, no reason. Someone I met was holding onto something for me.'

'Your days of waiting are over, Milton. Forget about it,' she continues, emotionlessly.

'Shit.' I mourn the loss of Annie and my glimpse. The last thing she said comes back to me. 'My friend said she'd been in the waiting room for sixty years. Is that normal?'

Tracey huffs audibly. 'No, not normal, but not unheard of. Most people get between six months and two years.'

'Anne Waits must have had a real naughty side if she amassed sixty years' worth of waiting,' I say, regretting our short time together even more.

'Sixty?' Tracey repeats. This obviously surprises her.

'Na, Hitler wouldn't have got sixty years. She more than likely sacrificed herself to Purgatory by choice.'

'Why would she do that?'

'For love, obviously.'

'Love?' I echo.

Tracey unleashes a squawked laugh, along with some spittle. 'Not with you.'

'I didn't think it was me!' I object.

'Sure you didn't, I can see your ego from here. The sort of love that someone sacrifices themselves for is mighty, unending and never wavers, not even in death. Not a chance meeting in a shitty waiting room,' she dismisses with brutal teenage honesty.

It's then I remember the old man who asked me for help this morning. I hadn't linked the wrinkled old-timer with the youthful Annie until now. He, like Annie, must have spent the last sixty years waiting to meet again. But while Annie sat waiting in perpetual youth, his waiting room was an Earth that aged and withered him. I really should have helped him. Maybe I wouldn't be dead now if I had. I feel a knot in my stomach as I think of them. I hope he lived a full and happy life without her. Sixty years of loneliness while old age claims your body would be tragic. 'At least I now know what Annie Waits was waiting for,' I mumble.

'What?' Tracey questions.

'Oh, nothing.'

The silence in the elevator is thick and oppressive; it feels like the walls are designed to absorb every sound made in the small space. 'What do you do round here, Tracey?' I ask to fill the amplified absence of noise.

'Temp,' she mutters back.

'You what?'

'Temp work, I'm a temporary worker. Minimum wage and all that.'

'Purgatory has temporary workers?'

'You bet. Millions of us. Shit-load of admin to do up here.'

'What are the hours like?' I continue my pointless questioning.

'Shocking! Eighty-five-hour weeks are standard.'

I offer a sympathetic frown. 'That's intense.'

'It's slave labour.'

'At least you're young,' I say, old before my time. 'You won't be stuck here your whole life; you'll move up and on soon enough. How long have you been doing it?'

'Six hundred years... ish,' she answers without flinching.

'Bloody hell. That's a shift.' Nothing compared to my Narration, mind; I wonder if everyone works like that in the Afterlife. But I don't want to get my Narration in trouble so instead I search for the next island in this polite back and forth. 'Holidays any good?'

Her terminally bored expression softens. 'Now they do give us that. Three years straight to do as we wish.'

'Good vacation.'

'Not compared to the 2,000 years we have to work to earn it, but yeah I need the break.'

'Three years,' I repeat. 'What do people do with that much time off?'

Tracey lifts herself from the back of the chair and leans against the glass wall to my left. 'Most go to Heaven, for a bit of divine R & R and all that. Some take a three-year-out backpacking trip round Earth, you know, three-dollar hotels, yurts, stables and all that. They all think they're being *so* original, but go round the same temples, get hammered at the same beach parties, write the same predictable wet poetry, grow the same grizzly beards and all smell like shit.'

'Travelling the world was my dream,' I say.

'You've got the beard for it,' she sniffs.

'The world is a book, and those who don't travel only read one page.' I quote the inside jacket of *Pictures of Cuba*. That sounded pretentious. Why did I say that – I must still be concussed.

Tracey barely suppresses a snorting giggle. 'A word of advice – don't go round Purgatory reciting pop quotes, especially ones by saints; people will think you're a dick. You don't want to go giving them any more reasons to send you to Hell, do you?'

Bloody hell, when did the dynamic change to her lecturing me? 'I guess not.'

'Speaking of which.' Her tone lightens. 'That's another holiday destination.'

My eyebrows leap. 'What is? Hell?'

'Yep.' A cheeky grin cuts across her face. 'Mostly upper management. *Just there to take in the sights*, they say. But we all know what that means – those fruity fucks get themselves a bit of Hell rough.'

'Hell rough?' Her grin's infectious. 'That doesn't sound very Christian.'

'You don't have to worry about that up here.'

'About what?'

'Christianity.'

'Why not?'

'Because it's a load of made-up bollocks. Surely you know that, right?' Tracey asks as if she's telling me that Spaniards like paella. 'It's obvious.'

'What do you mean *made up*? We're standing in Purgatory, how can it be made up?'

'Well…' Tracey pauses, frozen in thought, apparently deciding whether to tell her story or not. She stretches her back and, decision made, returns her sweaty back to the mirror. 'When I'm not carting heavy tourists around I work as an admin assistant in the Innovation of Religion department, where the guy who *made it all up* works. He's well known round here, actually.'

'Who?'

'Well, to give you a hint he's also the star of Christianity.'

'You mean…?'

'Yep.'

There's an obvious next question, but it's weird. I ask anyway. 'You work with Jesus?'

'Nah; not with,' Tracey answers, again with an impressive amount of ambivalence. 'He works at the other end of the office. I've never seen him.'

'You work in the same office as Jesus and you've never seen him?' I ask, ignoring the classroom of raised hands in my mind.

Tracey lets another weary sigh trickle from her nostrils. 'We don't deal with size in the same way as you. My office is a seven-day hike in every direction. And it's Barry Davis,' she adds, but I'm not sure why.

'What?'

'Barry Davis,' she repeats.

'Who's Barry Davis?'

'That's his name. He just used Yeshua to fit into early BC Judea.'

'Who's Yeshua?'

'It's the Hebrew name Barry used. The Greeks changed it to Jesus.'

My face crumples in contemplation. 'Jesus Christ's real name is Barry Davis?'

'Yep.'

'Christ. Are you sure we're not thinking of different people?'

'Of course we're not!' Her voice cracks. 'I have that sandal-wearing bastard's story of personal achievement shoved down my throat at every possible opportunity. We even have to take a course! BLBD they always say, *Be Like Barry Davis* – pisses me right off. He broke every law God holds dear creating that little utopia of his, and now he's Purgatory's poster boy.' She fixes a beady eye on me from under her greasy hair. 'Funny how the power barons change their minds about someone when it's suddenly in their favour. There was even talk that God would close the loop on the lie and officially adopt him.' Tracey snorts. 'But that's a level of office politics so far above my head it might as well be rammed up a seagull's arse.'

'He's not God's son?'

'Fuck no!' she scoffs.

I stretch my eyes wide as I process this information. 'Do people get to meet him then? Barry that is. Will I?'

'You wouldn't want to, mate. He's a corporate arsehole now. Your kind never see him anyway. Barry doesn't exactly fit the long hair and bangles image that you people have; he's more boardrooms and cufflinks nowadays. Your only chance would be to attend one of his insufferable *Breakfast with Barry* sessions, and I'd have to take you so that's not happening.'

'Shame, it would have been interesting.'

'Bullshit! He's an unoriginal corporate bitch. His lack of creativity is unmatched.' I think she's expecting some sort of reaction. I don't respond. Tracey lifts herself from the glass wall and stretches. I hear her bones crack. 'Okay, this is juicy, but you can't tell anyone I told you.' She doesn't wait for my agreement. 'Before taking his three-year sabbatical to Earth, Barry worked on some big God projects while temping in the IRD.'

'The IRD?'

'The Innovation of Religion Department. Keep up, Milton! First,' Tracey waggles one finger into her reflection, 'was an Egyptian god, Horus. Now, this guy, it was decided, would walk on water,' she counts on the same finger, 'heal the sick, restore sight to the blind, be born to a virgin and be known as the Son of God, and be crucified and resurrected; and so he was. Sound familiar?' She doesn't wait for an answer. 'The next god Barry worked on was Attis of Phrygia; a Greek god. Again born of a virgin, this time on 25 December, son of God, this one was named the Saviour, crucified and resurrected.' She leans to within an inch of the mirror, inspecting her nose with minute precision. 'Next big project, Krishna.' I know that one. I give a nod. 'I know, impressive right? As well as being hugely admired, Krishna was also visited at birth by star-guided wise men and shepherds, born to a virgin, son of God *and* named the Saviour, crucified and resurrected. And the final 400 years before Barry's holibobs were spent administering the progress of the Greek god Dionysus. Placed in a manger, virgin, December, son, saviour and crucified in 193 AD, obviously.' Her voice tenses as she squeezes a spot. 'Notice a theme?'

'You... um... really learnt a lot on that course.' I try to hide my revulsion as the pus hits the glass.

'I wish I didn't – trust me,' she says, her breath steaming the mirror.

I try to process the information and ignore the second spot she's picking at. 'Barry worked on all of those? That's still pretty impressive.'

'His contribution was about as impressive as the shit I took this morning! He sat in the corner filing papers; that's all. He stole the perfect divine persona from all those gods and played it out on Earth.'

'No wonder people took to him, sneaky fucker.'

Another yellow splatter hits the mirror. 'Yes!' Tracey cheers, happy that I finally seem to get the point. 'Gave Barry everything he needed to assemble Christianity like a sexy and seamless Frankenstein's monster. Gets dropped off in the Middle East on a plague run, made up an insultingly one-dimensional story about the birth of a god attended by shepherds and wise men, didn't even bother making up a childhood or adolescence – lazy bastard, sang his heart out about the Afterlife for three years, did a few magic tricks and got himself crucified.'

'And that was it?'

'Yep.'

'Hell of a marketing campaign. How many Christians are there?'

Tracey pivots from the wall. ''Bout two billion, give-or-take.'

'All that from a few antics in the Middle East 2,000 years ago?'

'Basically.' She shrugs. 'All he did was charm some barely educated desert dwellers. You did the rest.'

'I did?'

'No.' Tracey sighs. 'You people.' She speaks as if I'm slow. 'You people, created Christianity as it's known today.' Tracey stares up at the floors ticking over. 'Barry didn't need to create the finished religion, just plant the seed and let mankind do the rest.'

I frown into the mirror. 'What did we do?'

'You acted like corrupt maniacs is what. Christianity rode your pathetic crooked natures and inability to deal with death through the generations.' She leans back on the chair. 'My God, you people have an unparalleled flair for missing the point. I bet even Barry didn't see the Mormons coming, and miniature versions of the cross Barry was murdered on round your necks. Classic mankind.'

'That is a bit weird I guess,' I consider.

'Yep, bonkers.' Tracey gives a thoughtful grunt. 'I had a Middle Eastern motivational speaker in here the other day. Lovely guy. Tried for years to break into the US Christianity market, shit-load of money in it apparently. *Can you do it with an American accent?* they asked him.' She barks a laugh. 'An American accent! These idiots don't dare make a decision without referring to the teachings of a 2,000-year-old public speaker; but a man from the same background, who, as an added bonus, speaks with the benefit of 2,000 years of human experience, and they couldn't care less. Quirky fuckers. And ironic, considering Purgatory's PR department tries to send him back every 200 years or so to tour the Christian world and all he gets is mocked.'

'Send who? Barry? Jesus returned to Earth?'

Tracey can't hide a mischievous grin. 'Yeah, he did, eight or nine times. He got crucified another two times for impersonating Christ, burned as a witch – that was when he stopped walking on water – stoned to death by early settlers and thrown into slavery by a white Christian land owner in the States. Most of the other times he was just ignored for being weird, or sectioned.'

The floors tick by... 555... 556... 557... 'I can't believe Jesus walked amongst us.'

'And you didn't give a shit. It's the hype you people love, not the reality.'

'That's what I couldn't get over, it's too stupid. Although, the peace of mind of thinking there's life after death, would have been cool.'

'You got that now?' Tracey sniffs.

'A bit, I guess. Feels like more of the same really. Always thought my body would just rot and my mind would go black and still. No thought, no feeling, no opinion, no knowledge of anything. But hey, Earth's gone and I can still feel, see and smell. It's not the way all those negative realists said it would be. God knows why I believed them.'

'Cause you were suckered in by their latest religion, obviously.'

'No, I wasn't,' I protest, insulted that she obviously hasn't been listening to a word I've said.

'Yeah you were, you just said so.'

I slow my voice to allow her time to realise her mistake. 'I just said I wasn't a Christian.'

She matches my slow speech. 'So you don't believe in science?'

'Yeah, but science is real; Christianity isn't.'

Her eyebrows bob up. 'Is it?'

'Yes, of course it is.' I twist towards her, awkwardly. 'Isn't it?'

'You just said it yourself: you expected to die and rot. The fact that you're still very much breathing and not decomposing somewhat shits in the face of science. Don't you think?'

'I'm breathing because I have a hamster in my chest.'

She shoots me a surprised glance, but speaks without missing a beat. 'And you don't think a rodent living in your chest cavity sits somewhere outside the governing rules of science?'

'I guess so.'

'Not to mention you're currently sitting in, and are surrounded by, Purgatory, a place that does and doesn't exist, somewhere between Earth and the Heavens.'

'But... but... but,' I grasp, 'science is complicated, it's not... get born a virgin, get crucified and get resurrected, it's... it's complicated.'

'It *is* – the new religion had to be. Science was the biggest project ever taken on by the Innovation of Religion Department. I was one of millions of temp workers brought in to complete the new vision. Traditional religion was on the decline so, same as

Barry did with Christianity, at some point in your sixteenth century we planted the seed of science and we grew it from there.'

'My God! But some science must be true?'

'Obviously, it wouldn't be a good lie if there weren't some truth sprinkled in there for good measure. Biology does govern your body, just differently to your understanding. Laws of physics do govern reality and the universe, just a different reality and universe to the ones you think you're in. We fed you a different version of the truth, complicated enough to keep you interested, but not so difficult that the message couldn't be preached.'

'So the universe isn't... the universe?'

She rubs her temples. 'I really shouldn't be telling you this stuff. She stares into her own reflection for a second. 'Okay, no, the universe isn't trillions of galaxies, there isn't even one.' She flickers a bashful grin. 'The Milky Way doesn't exist – we fabricated it to keep you lot staring up while we pulled your trousers down. The solar system is true, sun, planets, etc., but the rest is just a very sophisticated light show on a big fucking screen. I can't wait for one of your rockets to fly straight into it, freak you right out.'

I feel the colour draining from me. 'So what's beyond the screen?'

Tracey heaves a weighty laugh. 'Now that's a question.' Her eyes drift up to the numbers. 'Well, good talk, chief. I'm going to need the chair, I'm afraid. Don't worry, though, we'll find you another one.'

I turn cumbersomely in the chair. 'Don't worry, I can walk from here...' The ping of the lift doors interrupts me. Tracey leans down, her face close to mine. 'Don't mention anything I've told you.' With no further words and zero ceremony she shoves the chair aggressively towards the doors. Twisting back, I see that they've opened to reveal a never-ending blue sky. I don't have time to bale or even grab the wheels before Tracey levers the chair forward and catapults me into free-fall.

X

10 hours 8 minutes after

Ten minutes of screaming is exhausting. I stop. Still no sign of the ground. This is going to be one hell of an impact. Maybe tucking myself into a ball or holding my nose will help. Or aiming for water. I once read a book on surviving extreme situations – it had a section on jumping into water from great heights. Apparently, clenching your buttocks on entering the water is essential... to... well... stop the water entering you.

A few minutes of buttock clenching becomes boring. Maybe I'm damned to fall for ever... that could get tedious. Or maybe I'm being sent back to Earth. The reward for an average life? Not bad enough to go to Hell and too indifferent to go to Heaven, so back to Earth – with quite a bump it seems.

Just as I'm getting used to constantly popping ears, I notice I'm not alone. About six metres away is an old leather chair. I guess that's my replacement. I try to manoeuvre into its path. It's tricky, but I make progress adopting the pose of a rigor mortis flying squirrel. Then, using a method I'm going to call 'the double windmill', I get close enough to grasp the chair's back, sending both it and me into a wild spin. Clinging to the spiralling chair, I drag myself into the seat. That's unexpected – it has a seat belt. I heave the belt across my lap and lock it.

The spinning finally slows. I open my eyes and take in the chair. It's aged but not too shabby.

I stare down and see a flock of birds. I'm headed straight for them. They look like swans, but there's something about them – their legs are sticking up. I think they're flying upside down. I stare as I drop straight through the flock. They are, they're flying the wrong way up. Maybe it's a Purgatory thing.

Or maybe… shit, they're not flying upside down and I'm not falling. The swans are the right way up and I'm rising… to Heaven?

I soar at an incredible velocity. My progress hasn't slowed, not for a second. Odd how quickly your body can get used to travelling at speed. I haven't seen any other birds, or anything else, for what feels like ages. Except for a couple of wispy clouds, there's nothing. The light blue skies have turned deeper. The edge of Earth's atmosphere? Am I about to be launched into space? Can I breathe in space now?

And then something truly spectacular comes into

view. Sitting where the sky meets the cosmos is a vast rocky mass; it must be over a hundred miles across. 'What is that?' I murmur. Rugged rock formations jut out of a gloomy mist that sits low on its surface. It looks as dead and barren as the Moon, as if a many-billion-year-old meteor has simply ground to a halt at the edge of Earth's atmosphere. Far from being heavenly, I don't think I could imagine a more hellish scene. The star-spangled banner of space disappears behind it.

More chairs are approaching, all with high backs, red leather and passengers. One chair is gaining on me. Looking closer I see a gaunt, middle-aged man with no top on. He doesn't look well. 'Are you okay?' I call. Nothing. I'm not even sure he's conscious as he's slouched in his seat, his head flopping. 'Hey, can you hear me?' He lifts his frail head just enough to fix a pair of bloodshot eyes on me.

Then a flash of grey and he's gone. Bloody hell! What happened? Pieces of shattered chair fall round me, but the man is nowhere to be seen. I press deep into my chair and cling to the arms.

The meteor-like mass is closer. I can see the surface is covered with deep holes and I'm heading directly for one. Hundreds of chairs surround me like a flock of Victorian gentlemen migrating south for the winter. There's something else. More grey flashes. Like wolves, they dart between chairs, broken pieces of wood dropping like breadcrumbs.

What's happening? Whatever they are, there's a lot of them.

I catch a shadowy shape veering in and out of a tiny patch of cloud near me. It dips, leaving just a trace of its bulk gliding across the cloud cover. It moves towards a blonde woman. Suddenly, and with extraordinary power, a colossal shark with huge wings springs into view, its beating tail making an entire cloud spiral.

'Hey. Hey you,' I shout. 'Look out! It's coming for you.' She's too far away to hear.

Powerful jaws shake the chair savagely left and right then throw it into the air. The chair arches into the sky and falls. In a moment of desperation the woman flings herself from the chair onto the shark's back. She grabs at its fin. Like a bucking bronco it arches and dips, but the woman holds tight.

She doesn't see the second shark. Using one huge wing, it pivots with the power of a two-tonne baseball bat. Blindsided, the woman's limp body soars across the sky directly into the path of another shark. In one instinctive movement the third hunter jerks its head to the left and swallows her whole. It's the kind of animalistic brutality David Attenborough should be describing. I'd probably be enthralled by this savage waltz if it weren't happening directly in fro— Oh shit, one just darted past me. The air from its wings ruffles my hair on the second pass. On the third it rams the back of my chair, sending me into a spin. I dig my nails into the arms. There's a jolt as the shark grips the chair and shakes it like a dog with a rag doll... then... nothing. An eerie stillness as my chair floats forward. It let go. Why?

Oh fuck... that's why. Metered beats of huge wings track me, its massive grey snout inches from my face, savouring the meal to come. This is it. I wait for it to strike. The creature silently fixes one huge eye on me, its mouth open, displaying two lines of grim razored teeth. They grind as a muscular grimace runs along their length. I'm trembling uncontrollably. Its gigantic eye pierces me, lays me bare.

My nose is bleeding. Did he do that?

The eye narrows. It's smelt blood, it's going to tear me apart. I clamp my eyes shut. I can't breathe.

Where is it?

Waiting?

Nothing.

I open my eyes.

It's gone.

I breathe.

There's only the colossal rock looming above me, so close it feels like I'm coming into land on an alien planet.

Alongside me, hundreds of survivors of the shark-infested sky enter holes in the landmass, but none is heading for mine. My chair dips beneath a particularly jagged peak and plunges into the ground mist. Everything goes dark.

I'm still moving but can't make out where or how... or why! The hole feels vast. I tentatively call out, 'Hello?' My voice echoes down a tunnel, an immense burrow drawing me deeper and deeper, until, suddenly, light floods in.

My nuts leap into my stomach, my stomach jumps into my chest and my lungs disappear into my brain as the chair slams the brakes on. It hovers, I feel a short sharp shock, then nothing.

I open my eyes. I'm sprawled on a rough dirty rock surrounded by pieces of shattered chair. I must have hit the surface hard. 'Fuck me!' My back twinges. I have whiplash in places only discussed in medical journals and adult movies. Stumbling to my feet, I let out a deep groan; my neck and back are throbbing. I shake my head.

An inspection reveals a colossal cave. The meteor is entirely hollow. The sides curve up to a vast dome that disappears into gloom in every direction. The surface is cold and damp but thankfully level. There's mist in here, too. It sits at knee-level and flows gently towards the hole, then like a mystical waterfall tumbles over the edge. The cavern echoes with dripping water, so much dripping water it creates a low, constant rumble that fills the massive space.

Where the hell now? Am I expected to stay here? I kick through the debris of my broken chair.

Thirty minutes pass... slowly. Trying to build a shelter from the chair parts is a dismal failure, so instead I make do lying on the cushions.

It takes me a few moments to realise something is different. It's subtle, but something has definitely changed. Rolling from the cushions, I crouch, letting the mist fall round my shoulders. I see it. Fifty metres ahead a small patch of mist is glowing brighter than the rest, and moving directly towards me. 'What the...?' The anonymous glow stalks me at a fast walking pace but smoothly like a fish through water. It's fascinating and eerie. Currently it's more eerie. My heart pounds against my rib cage. No need to panic. Just keep sight of the glow.

Wait a minute, I don't have a heart, so what's pounding in my chest? 'Penfold!' Unbuttoning the long dress jacket, I realise he's ramming the other side of the door in my chest. It's like something has triggered, telling him it's time to bale out. Grasping hold of the tiny handle, I open the door. Spring loaded, Penfold Fingerstick jumps from my chest. 'Come back here, you little bastard,' I shout as my furry companion disappears into the mist. My Narration's warning leaps into my mind – I need him in there. I wait, frozen, for... something to happen. But nothing does. I feel fine. My breaths roll without faltering. Peering into my chest I can see that the wheel still turns, driven by free-flowing blood. I edge the door shut. Apparently I'm okay for the minute.

The frosty mist cools my face, a mist that seems to be glowing brighter, a lot brighter. I fall backwards as a luminescent orb passes inches above my face. The light is intense – it blinds me.

My vision returns in time to see the sphere disappearing into the mist. What the hell was that? With a quick sprint I catch up as the orb glides gracefully through the shallow haze. 'What are you?' I move closer. There's nothing inside the light that I can see. No eyes, no mouth, no nose, no brain, just more light. I can see straight through to the other side. What is it? A scout sent to guide me? Like salmon swimming upstream, it seems to act on instinct. There's nothing propelling it forward or showing it the way, but still the sphere follows its course, like there's something calling to it, drawing it in.

We trek together for what feels like an hour. 'There's a lot of walking in Purgatory,' I say to the ball of light. 'I hope this doesn't become a theme.'

The orb doesn't answer. It's not very chatty.

'Assuming we're still in Purgatory,' I confirm, craning my neck to scan this immense Gothic space. As my eyes accustom to the darkness, I spot silhouettes, moving like insects in and out of burrows. In fact, the high corners of this cave are crawling with life. They're not small either – some of these creatures are definitely larger than me. God, I hope they stay up there. 'What the fuck are they?' I whisper to the orb.

The more I stare, the more shapes appear, hundreds ghosting through the dusk.

The orb has got ahead of me. 'Wait!' I call, more in desperation than expectation. But it works – the ball freezes. 'Oh, thanks,' I say, giving the ball an apprehensive stare. Can it understand me?

Catching up, I realise it's stopped because of a wall. The other end of the cave, I guess. My first instinct is to look up to the dark corners again. The creatures are still there. Dust trickles down the rock wall. I imagine sharp claws moving large muscular bodies along tight ledges somewhere above.

The ball hovers at my side like a friendly spectre. 'What now? There's nothing here, just the other side of the cave. Are we in the wrong place? What sort of guide are you?' I squint upwards. 'We need to get moving. I don't know what's up there, and I don't want to find out.' Tentatively, I give the orb a gentle shove. A violent pulse shoots from the ball, knocking me from my feet.

I shake my head. 'Sorry,' I stutter. 'Lesson learnt: you don't like touching.' But it's gone. The sphere has taken off round the edge of the cave. I try to follow, but something's wrong. My chest is being crushed, tightening every time I breathe out. I can't lose the orb; it's a rubbish guide, but I don't have any other options. Keeping a good distance between me and my volatile companion, I force myself to move. What's happening to me? I can hardly focus. If I get another shock I won't be getting up. Using the slick cave rock for support, I limp along, closing the gap on the ball of light. It's slowed, possibly to accommodate me, but maybe that's just wishful thinking. My God this hurts. It feels like a massive sink hole has opened up inside me.

I stumble behind the ball of light for what feels like hours but is probably only minutes. My legs give way. I drop to the floor. My body is imploding, my legs are so weak I don't think I can stand. I try, but they buckle under me. With my cheek pressed against the cold floor, my body is swallowed up by the mist. All I can do is watch the ball of light effortlessly glide away, its glow disappearing with it. But something remains. The orb's sensitive edges have left a shimmering residue in the mist. All around me the mist takes on the same glow. I'm either hallucinating – a distinct possibility – or something significant is happening. Calling on every last bit of strength, I peel my face from the floor and struggle to my knees. A trail of sparkling mist leads my fragmented vision to the threshold of an archway almost as high as this cavern. Please, God, let that be the exit.

XI

11 hours 34 minutes after

Dragging myself to my feet, I limp forward. Through the smog of my failing eyesight I glimpse movement in the arch. Now I'm sure I'm hallucinating. I screw my eyes up, breathe and look again. It's alive!

The walls are beating with flesh, blood and bone. An organic vision of limbs, lungs, arms, legs, heads and brains. Thousands of the lightest blue eyes, hundreds of thousands of twitching ears and millions of gleaming white teeth, all twist in and out of holes in the ancient grey rock.

The orb is waiting, I think, telling me to go through. Do I trust it? Do I have a choice? The macabre exit terrifies me, but I'm too weak to stay here. Forcing a deep gasp from my barely functioning lungs, I stumble forward.

Sensing my presence, the vast pillars stir. Inquisitive tentacles twisted with human body parts edge towards me. They're going to grab me. They move too fast. I'm engulfed. I'm off my feet! Can't fight, I'm too weak. My head swims as in seconds I'm a hundred feet up, held tight like a fly in a web. My broken body at the will of this creature.

Smaller worm-like tentacles force their way up my jacket sleeves and trouser legs and strip the clothes from my body. Enveloped, I feel powerless; only my nose and mouth are clear. I fight to stay conscious. There's a crack from my chest. I think they just ripped the little wooden door open. At first the inquisitive worms just circle the gaping wound, but all it takes is a couple of sniffs and they dive in. Oh God, they're going inside me! Adrenaline gives me enough of a kick for a brief struggle against the writhing mass but it's no use. Even at full strength I'd never break free.

I retch as the appendages move round my internal organs, making me shudder and shiver with bone-shaking intensity. The uninvited enemas tear into my defenceless organs, my skin stretches and bones groan. They creep inside my spine. I judder. The ferocity of my movement is enough to shake the writhing limbs from my face. I see what's going on. I wish I hadn't. My liver is being expelled from the now huge hole in my chest. 'No,' I gasp as it disappears into the twisting mass of body-part tentacles, followed by four further bloody organs. They look important. What if this beast of Purgatory is designed to harvest the bodies of those that pass underneath? They're pulling me apart! 'Stop!' I protest weakly.

I glimpse the vast pillars of intertwined body parts.

How else could such a creature exist without poaching body parts from those foolish enough to stumble into its grip? This grisly monster is going to hollow me out like an octopus gutting a Christmas turkey. Got to escape. With renewed strength I yank at my fleshy shackles. A few tentacles lose their grip. Sensing victory, I squirm and pull even harder. Instantly, an ominous groan rumbles through the pillars on both sides. Like a swarm of angry bees, hundreds of tentacles burst free and surge towards me. They hit hard, and in seconds I'm bound tight, completely powerless in the middle of a ball of securely packed eels. I hang, helpless, feeling the tentacles writhing inside me, in this hot, humid slime. I gag as it fills my nose and mouth. It reeks. I'm suffocating.

Only I'm not. I'm alive, whatever alive means, in a kind of living cocoon. Weirdly, I don't feel weak; I'm clear-headed and oddly sanguine about this traumatic situation. After a while, it just turns into another boring damp place in which I've been trapped.

Long after that epiphany, and after my entire body has gone numb, the worms begin to retreat. I can't feel them inside me any more. I sense tentacles lowering me to the floor. There's a sharp bump and the movement stops. I wait for something to happen. Nothing does.

I try to shift my position. I can move. I push at what feels like tightly woven soft tissue all around me; it gives way. The slimy substance is difficult to grip, but pressing in every direction I gradually hollow out a larger and larger space. Thrusting my fist as far as possible into the thick pale limbs, I think I can feel freedom. I twist my hand in a circular motion. It definitely feels like fresh air. I push my head and then shoulders through the tentacles. It takes longer than I expect, but finally, like a newborn reptile hatching from an egg, I slip from my slimy prison. Naked and covered in embryonic gunk, I lie on the floor. The light stuns my eyes as I scrabble like an ungainly doe in the slick substance. I plead with my vision to clear and, as it does, I see the tentacles receding into the rock wall, like snakes retreating to the roots of two almighty trees.

XII

12 hours after

The sun is really bright. I can hear seagull cries echoing round me and a fresh breeze cools the foul-smelling slime coating my body. Wiping it from my chest, I inspect the area that the tentacles hollowed out. The gaping hole is completely healed! Breathing deeply, I feel whole again. Did the tentacles fix me? What about on the inside?

I rub my hands together. A gasp suspended somewhere between religious experience and a baffling magic trick tumbles from my lips. I turn my hand over, and then back again. The three fingers sliced off by the car door have regrown. I stare confounded at the new digits. I push my fingers together, relishing a long-lost sensation.

This side looks more like a weather-withered cliff than the other. It still has a stark white colouring but the smooth finish has disappeared, replaced by jagged rock. I'm high up, perched on a large peninsula jutting out from the cliff like a Roman emperor's plinth. Using one of the large stones scattered round the clearing, I push myself to my feet and test my balance. Bracing myself against the wind, I stand and breathe in the full beauty of the scene. The sheer cliff that surrounds the outcrop must plummet fifty metres to the coast. From there, endless turquoise ocean fades to a luminous horizon in every direction.

Was that a cough? Still naked, suddenly I feel very exposed. I swivel to face the noise, but all I see is the gate and cliff side. The gate still throbs and moves but no one else has passed through. Only my orb waits patiently on the other side. Now that it's led me here, I think its job is done.

There's another, accentuated cough. I look towards the sound, somewhere amongst the large rocks protruding from the cliff face, but there's nothing there. I turn to the sea, scrutinising the area as I go.

'I know,' comes a sharp voice from behind, 'I can see it too. Disgusting, isn't it?' The voice is far closer than I expect. I wheel round to find the half-metre frame of my Narration standing just a few paces away. He nonchalantly glances at everything God blessed me with as it swings into his eye-line. 'Please cover that,' he grimaces, 'there's a lady present.'

I cup my goods with one hand and shade my brow with the other as the harsh sun reflects from the brilliant white rock. 'Narration,' I say numbly, 'is that you?'

'Yes, Milton, it is me.'

He's back in his glistering red cloak.

'How are you here?'

He barks a laugh and bounces the brass tip of his ceremonial cane on the hard rock. 'He watched us get sucked into an interdimensional portal,' he glances to the space behind him, 'and he asks us how we got here – bigger picture, Milton!' he advises, with that intimidating authority of his.

I guess that means he's brought his little group with him.

'Aren't you meant to be narrating your next life?'

'What?' His authority slips. 'I know you're not good in the heat, Arik-boke, but I have larger issues to deal with.'

'What larger issues?' I say.

He snaps back to me. 'Yes, Milton,' he almost hisses, 'thank you for enquiring, we were meant to be narrating our next life, but instead we seem to be here, talking to you, *again*, in Heaven! We hate fucking Heaven! It's all hot and sweaty and disorganised.' His head leaps to the left for a second. 'And Kazuo has allergies. Bless you, Kazuo.'

'This is Heaven?' My pulse leaps. I can't suppress the smile.

'Of course this is Heaven.' He raises his arms to the sky, displaying the pitifully tiny loincloth beneath his cloak. 'Where did you think you were? On holiday in Greece?' Fatigued, his arms slump back down. 'It's hot enough.'

Awkwardly turning to face the horizon, I try my best not to point my naked arse directly at him. 'I didn't know what to expect,' I consider.

'Sun, sea and sand, the standard,' he coldly summarises, 'what you bottom-feeders work all your little lives for.'

I ignore his attitude. 'This is Heaven.' I appreciate the moment. It is pretty momentous, after all, even if my Narration seems intent on ruining it. I let warm rays soak into my entire body. It really relaxes me.

Peering back towards the gate, I notice a pile of gaudy purple rags at the base of one of the pillars. My suit spewed out by the intrusive tentacles. 'Do you mind if I put some clothes on?' I ask. 'I'm feeling a little exposed.'

'Go on then.' He waves his cane. 'I think we've all had enough of that pale milk-bottle body of yours. It's bad enough that we had to see it on screen for all those years, but in real life...' He visibly shivers.

Still cupping myself, I cautiously sidle up to the gate. The last thing I need is to be grabbed by this grisly fucker again. Glancing left then right, I take my chance. The gate doesn't react. I collect my clothes without further incident. They're torn and a long way from their dazzling beginnings. In fact, the jacket is too shredded to wear, but the trousers are passable, so I button them up and go topless.

Something seems to be agitating the Narration. With his head down and shoulders hunched, he's babbling to himself, every now and then turning his head just a little to receive the opinions of his broken mind. I take the opportunity to investigate the far side of the plateau. I spot the top of a small path nestled between the edge of the gate and the cliff face. The barely perceptible trail twists down the steep cliff side until it disappears at the edge of a long sandy beach. The path looks dangerous, but if I take it slowly I should be fine. Plus there don't seem to be any other options. The beach is stunning. That's definitely my kind of Heaven. I wonder if there's a bar.

I glance back to my Narration; he's still deep in debate. Why is he here? Is he meant to be coming with me? Do I want him to?

Approaching slowly, I notice that his hands aren't moving. 'Hey, you're managing to keep your fingers still. You beat it, congratulations!'

He seems annoyed at me interrupting his conversation. 'Thanks,' he hisses aggressively without looking at me.

'Are you all right?' I venture. 'You seem a bit agitated.'

His head jerks towards me. 'Agitated,' he exclaims, 'agitated, *agitated*. Milton Pitt thinks I'm agitated,' he straightens himself and declares. 'Well,' he scowls, 'maybe that's because we've spent the last five hours being lectured on the importance of the sacred role of the Narration,' he bellows, 'by God!' This outpouring of emotion seems to have been too much for the little man as he crumples to the floor, his eyes welling up. 'A perfect 60,000-year blemish-free record, I narrated on the Grand Duchess Anastasia,' he begins to blubber, 'and then, Milton Pitt, a nobody, comes along and destroys everything.' He points a crooning finger at me. 'That's what you do, isn't it? You destroy everything, you monster.'

My first instinct is to cut and run for the path. The last thing I need in Heaven is these amateur dramatics. But given I am in Heaven, I guess I should show some more compassion, at least briefly. I sigh. I'll comfort him then go. 'I'm sorry you got disciplined by God, but I think you're a great Narration, I'm sure you were just unlucky, it wasn't your fault.'

Like a crack of lightning his mood turns from sadness to anger. 'I know it wasn't our fault – it was your fault, you laboursome moron. How many did you steal?'

'I didn't.' I back away, hands raised. 'How many what?'

'How many pages of your life did you steal from us?' He emphasises every word.

The pages I stuffed in my pocket? That's what this is about. 'Um... four or five, I think,' I mutter. I don't like the way this is going – should have just run. I won't make that mistake again.

'You stole your entire last day on Earth! It is my divine role as a Narration to write a full and accurate account of a human's life and send all that knowledge in the white smoke up the chimney so that God, my boss, may inhale it and immediately know every moment. But he didn't know every moment of your damn life, because you stole the last day! You stood in front of him and he had no idea how you died. There's one rule in this place: don't make the boss look like a prick. You royally screwed us, Milton Pitt.' Threat ripples through the Narration's words as he grips the top of his cane.

'But, but...' I repeat, trying to process this information. 'I haven't even met God!'

'Of course you've met God,' he cuts back, 'he meets all of you, even the ones that don't believe in him. You even watched him inhale the white smoke and still you didn't realise you were in the presence of God, you simpleton.'

My mind suddenly ticks. 'The freshen-up guy?'

'Obviously, the freshen-up guy,' he goads.

'That was God?'

'Obviously, obviously, obviously.' He bangs his cane on the floor repeatedly, then swivels away from me. 'How is this news to him?'

'And the hit he took from that huge shisha pipe was the white smoke from your fireplace?'

He turns back to me with a fatigued sigh. 'Yes.'

My nose crumples. 'Why the fuck was he in that toilet?'

He shrugs. 'Just one of those off-beat quirks. Gives him the chance to interact with humans when they're least expecting it. It's just his godly way.'

I sense his anger ebbing a little.

'Didn't seem very godly when he sprayed me in the eyes,' I grumble jovially.

'You probably didn't avert your gaze,' the Narration returns, then smirks at his invisible audience.

'So God uses cheat notes?' I feel the need to clarify.

'Of course. One being couldn't judge the entirety of humanity without using a few tricks.'

'I guess not, now I think about it he did seem a little confused, I just assumed he'd been drinking.'

'He probably had,' the Narration murmurs.

I slump onto a nearby boulder. 'Bloody hell,' I exhale. 'God hangs around in manky toilets smoking the stories of people's lives. Who'd have thought it? I guess I really did screw you over. I'm sorry. I didn't think a few pages would matter. What can I do to make it up to you?' I offer an apologetic smile. 'I noticed a beach down by the coast. We could see if they do drinks or something. I think that would cheer us all up.' Glancing around, I try my best to include all of my Narration's people.

The Narration takes a thoughtful moment to wipe his loose sleeve round his sweaty brow. A sigh softens his expression and his tight shoulders relax just a little. 'We're all to blame.' His voice takes on a sympathetic tone. 'And it's not what *I* want, it's what we owe to God,' he says calmly. 'We've paid our debt; now you've got to pay yours.'

'What?' I stutter. 'Me? I'm in Heaven; you can't punish me.' My eyes dart to the track. 'You're going to take Heaven away from me, aren't you?'

'Not me,' he emphasises, 'but you're right, you won't be staying.'

That's it. I'm running. Maybe I can find somewhere on the coast to hide out. But it's the Narration who's in motion, not me. With pinpoint venom he strikes the side of my knee with his cane. Something behind my knee-cap cracks.

I howl as a ball of pain swells in my leg. I try to balance but only manage for a second before collapsing to the floor. 'Why the fuck...?' I screech as a second, stronger wave of agony reverberates through me.

The Narration, now returned to set position, coolly leans back on his cane. 'We've watched you for twenty-six years, Milton. I know when you're about to run,' he informs without a hint of remorse. 'I've got 60,000 years of experience with you people running away – you did it all the time in the old days. Sixty thousand years that now mean nothing, until you've paid your debt.'

But I'm not finished: my impulse to preserve my Heaven is still greater than my urge for self-preservation. At the end of his little speech I grab hold of the bottom of his cane and ram it into the bridge of his little button nose. Stunned, he reels back with a cry that tells me I hit my spot. In a second I've used the cane again to swipe his feet from under him, bringing my Narration down hard on the boulder. Now I need to put some distance between us. Dropping all of my weight onto my good leg, I grab hold of one of his skinny ankles, spin him once, then fling his stunned, diminutive body to the far end of the clearing. His tiny frame glides through the air like a Chihuahua thrown by a quarterback. He lands heavily on the rock surface before sliding to a dusty halt. Not the kindest way to treat the being that has watched over me my entire life, but I want to stay here. Besides, he started it.

Using the boulder I just poleaxed him from, I prop myself up to assess his condition. He's not moving. I look to the sandy track. It's going to be a nightmare with this leg, but it's now or never.

A pained cough comes from the Narration's direction. Another cough, this time turning into a shell-shocked laugh. 'Woah-wee!' he yells, stumbling back to his feet. 'That cleared the sinuses. I did not see that one coming, Milton Pitt. Bravo!' He couldn't sound more proud if he tried. 'Look at the distance I travelled – that's got to be some sort of record!' As he speaks he slips off his dusty cloak, leaving him dressed only in his loincloth. 'Well, Milton, it appears we have a fight on our hands,' he says, taking a handful of dirt and rubbing it into his palms. He bares his teeth and crouches, ready to attack. 'What?' He's suddenly distracted by one of his group. 'You're betting on him!' the Narration yells. 'Lady Jane, you are a traitorous harlot!... I don't care if you like his face... What?... No, I won't promise not to punch it. In fact, that's exactly what I'm going to do!' His wild eyes dart back to me.

'...Give me a moment, I'm thinking,' he mutters to the assembly beside him. The Narration tilts his head like a carpenter sizing up a job. 'Okay, put me down for ten seconds, and three... You heard me, all three,' he stresses with a dismissive flick of the wrist. 'Now shut up! I need to focus.' He takes three rapid breaths, exhales slowly, then, like a mini tribesman going to war, he charges. I'm just able to set myself as he accelerates into a huge leap that propels him through the air directly towards my face. I grab him before he connects, but his momentum sends us both tumbling to the ground. In a flash he's up and strikes me with three shockingly brutal punches to the face. Before I even open my eyes he has already locked his legs round my left shoulder and I hear a very unnatural pop immediately followed by thunderous pain. He rolls away, turns and comes again. Stumbling to my feet, I attempt to seize him, but only my right arm obeys; my left is dislocated. He evades my limited attack and plants a two-footed kick into my injured knee. With a pathetic yelp I slump back to the floor. But the assault isn't over. Latching his entire body onto my good arm, he twists my hand viciously. An unstoppable wail vomits from me as immobilising pain sensors light up throughout my entire body.

'I submit, I submit!' I shout, but he doesn't yield. An unbearable burst of pain explodes in one of my knuckles. I hear the visceral snaps of serious damage being done. Adrenaline ignites within me. 'What are you doing?' I cry. 'Get the fuck off!' I flail the assaulted arm around, flipping myself over and slamming him down on the floor, anything to free myself, but his grip doesn't give, in fact he barely seems to notice. The appalling pain returns a second, and a third time. Summoning my last morsels of energy, I lift the Narration as high as my injured limbs can bear, then ram him down onto a boulder. He gasps as I wind him just enough to loosen his hold. Pivoting my body, I fling my arm upwards, sending the Narration tumbling through the air. I flop onto the grubby rock floor. He bounces twice, before expertly righting his footing and sliding to a standing stop. I've got nothing left. If he attacks again I'm done for. He turns his head to the side and spits out three large chunks of something. He hollers a laugh back to his band. 'All three! What was my time? What? That was never fifteen seconds. Your timings are out. Recount!'

Lying motionless, I watch the Narration stomp over to his starting position to apparently confront the timekeeper. As he falls out of focus, something closer drops in. Three freshly cut fingers sit like half-eaten sausages discarded from a grisly chef's table. I raise my hand. The sight of my three stark white knuckle bones protruding from the torn flesh of my fingers is too much. My vision flickers, I slump to the ground, darkness engulfs me.

My eyes snap open with a jolt of pain. 'Argh!' I cry. With his gleaming robe back across his shoulders, the Narration stands over me, both hands on my dislocated shoulder.

'Stop,' I flinch, 'please stop hurting me!'

'You're not going to try and run again, are you?'

'No.'

'Then hold still. I've almost fixed this,' he says, feeling the swollen contours of my shoulder. Before I have time to object, my shoulder snaps back into its socket.

'There we go, all fixed,' he nurses, as if he wasn't the one who inflicted it. 'He always was a fainter,' he jokes off to the side.

'Get the fuck away from me, you little psycho!' I shove him.

'That's a mean thing to say,' he pouts, taking a couple of steps back.

'What do you expect? You bit my fucking fingers off!' I raise my broken hand only to notice it's wrapped in a blood-stained bandage.

'I did my best with the binding,' he ignores my outburst, 'but I only had my loincloth so it's a bit makeshift I'm afraid.'

'My new fingers,' I mourn, 'I only had them back a few minutes.' It's exactly the injury pattern

I sustained in the car door. Somehow I'm guessing that's not a coincidence. I edge back to lean on the boulder and hold my broken hand close to my chest.

'God giveth, and God taketh away – literally,' he says as if all thoughts of violence have been banished from his mind. 'If it helps,' he continues, 'I would have had to remove those fingers at some point anyway. That level of regeneration is only for the residents of Heaven.'

'Shit,' I groan. 'Please don't send me to Hell,' I feel compelled to say. 'If Heaven is this crap I can't image how bad Hell is gonna be.'

'No, no, no,' the Narration chuckles, 'you've lived a pretty good life. Well,' he wavers, 'not a bad life anyway. Boring, maybe, even if you did steal my papers and throw me by my foot. No, your life has been based around a pretty sound philosophy. We don't just send people to Hell willy-nilly.'

'So where do you want me to go?' I say, suppressing another wave of pain.

'Not me,' he stresses. 'God! You owe God the day you stole.'

'What? But I don't have the papers any more,' I plead breathlessly.

'He doesn't want the papers, Milton. If it was that easy, don't you think I would have just gone and retrieved them from Annie Waits? No, what you need to do is relive the day that doesn't exist.'

How does he know about Annie? Wait... 'Are you sending me back to Earth?'

'I think he's got it,' he announces. 'You'll relive it, every moment, and we'll be narrating every moment with you, again! Then everything will be...' The Narration motions to continue speaking but a movement catches his peripheral vision. Following his line of sight, I notice something at the gate's entrance. It's the luminescent orb passing under the arch. Sensing its presence, the tentacles sweep down to surround the glowing sphere, but more warily, caressing rather than imprisoning, as if caught in a strange seduction. I can clearly see human body parts mixing with the light, each independently alive, and more than that, seeming to have its own goal, like a horde of competing males jostling for position. I even see two shoulderless arms wrestling each other.

Piece by piece, flesh by bone, like planets drawn into the orbit of a new star, everything gravitates towards the orb. A heart, stomach, spine, skull and brain have all gathered in the light, and following closely behind, ribs, arms and legs jostle for position. A skeleton forms, a ribcage lantern, which dims as a protective new skin is pulled over it before it disappears, immersed in a ball of swirling tentacles.

The ball of limbs moves towards us. At just a few metres, like a blooming flower, it slowly opens to unveil its creation. A female body, the size of a fully formed adult. The naked skin crackles and steams as it cools.

With her back to me, just two tentacles coil round the arms. The head hangs limp and out of sight. I'm not even sure she's conscious.

The tentacles release. Using my one good hand and one good leg, I propel myself across the small space between us. I reach out and her slender body falls into my arms. I force my lacerated hand to cradle the delicate base of her bald head.

'It's her,' I whisper. Holding her tightly, I wipe the thin film of fluid from her face and head. I see her properly for the first time. I was right – her face is otherworldly. Is that why I remembered her so vividly?

'Ah, there she is,' the Narration purrs sentimentally. 'Your Heaven, just as your glimpse predicted.'

Her cheekbones protrude far further than any I've seen before. They rise up round the sides of her hairless head in perfect symmetry and disappear somewhere behind her ears. From these distinctive ridges, soft skin slopes to a delicate chin as if she's been crafted by an artist working way ahead of his or her time. Her head isn't stubbled or rough; it's soft, no different from the skin on her cheek or neck.

'Don't worry, she'll be fine here without you.' Suddenly the Narration is behind me and, using his cane, has me in a choke hold. 'You two will have your love, but not yet.' He breathes heavily on the side of my face. I don't even have time to look again before the light fades. As I fall into deep darkness, I hear his softly spoken words whispered into my ear. 'Don't forget your top pocket, Mr Pitt.'

XIII

1 hour 34 minutes before

Everything is dark and everything is quiet.

The clock ticks over to 7.30am. I fumble for the snooze button. Finally, I manage to turn off 'Waterloo Sunset'. Goddamn, I think I've turned the snooze off. I'm actually feeling quite alert for this time in the morning so it may not be a problem. I don't even have a hangover. How the hell did that happen? The amount I drank last night I should have a rhino behind the eyes. I'm going to drink that brand of beer more, or was it wine?

As I stretch my extremities to every corner of the bed, a strange squawk escapes my lips. That was unexpected. I roll over to check if I've woken my hamster. Nope, the lazy little bastard is still sound asleep. 'Penfold!' I croak. 'Penfold, are you awake?' Nothing. Lazy bastard. I rub my eyes, and pull away to inspect my little fingers. I feel like I dreamt about them.

I can't believe how fresh I feel. This is great,

especially considering how bad this bed smells. I sniff the pillow. When did I wash my bedding last? Everything smells like vomit. Flipping onto my side, I make the most of the last few, lingering minutes of peace before I have to get up for work. My television is on. Apparently, I checked the football scores on teletext last night. Spurs 2 Liverpool 1 – we needed that.

I sniff the air. That's not the pillow; there's something worse in here. Shuffling to the side of the bed, I find the culprit. Is that sick in my bin? Oh dear God. 'It *is* sick,' I call out to Penfold, who still hasn't risen.

I stare vacantly at the book beneath the bin. *Pictures of Cuba* lies open. Gingerly, I lift the bin. There's a halo of sick circling Ernest Hemingway's Havana home – fitting, I guess. Even though time is short I let the limitless possibilities this book evokes wash through my veins for a moment. The experiences I'd have, the people I'd meet, the women I'd meet!

There's a rustling at the end of the bed. 'Penfold? Is that you? You sneaky little bastard. How did you get out of your cage?' Glancing up, I'm dazzled by light from the gap in the curtains. I squint as coloured bars bounce round my eyes, creating a female shape. A trick of the light surely. I blink rapidly, close my eyes, breathe and try to clear my vision. I open my eyes. The figure remains.

Someone's there – cold reality shudders through me. I freeze. Though nervous breaths tremble from my lips, I feel calm. How is it possible? Who is she? The ghostly figure stands, unmoving in the moment. How can this be anything more than imagination? But my imagination isn't this good. I rub my eyes, but still she stands, silhouetted by the morning sunshine. Did I pull last night? How did I forget that? I breathe and squint at the shadows of her form. No doubting it, she's there, standing with her back to me, at the end of my bed, naked. Where did she come from? How did I not see her? Was she lying on the floor? My eyes work their way up her body, fighting hard to remain on course until they break through the scattered rays of light bouncing hypnotically from a completely bald head.

I need to see her face, maybe it'll jog my memory. I unstick my lips. 'Hello?'

She says nothing.

I try again. 'Hello?'

With delicate poise, first her head turns, led by wide eyes. Taking the cue, her shoulders, hips and feet follow. 'Hello,' she greets with an emotionless expression. Her face is otherworldly, but familiar, very familiar.

'Um, hi,' I just about muster, 'did we meet at the pub?'

A smile softens her full lips as she shakes her head. 'Heaven,' her voice barely audible.

'Heaven,' I mimic like a man being visited by an angel.

'Don't rush to me, I'll wait,' she whispers with resonating meaning and lowers her head. Morning sunlight leaps from the soft contours of her head. Instinctively, my eyes snap shut. As quickly as they close, they open. I'm lying on the bed. She's gone.

Was I dreaming? It seems lighter, like time has moved on. I glance at the clock. *7.45am*. Quarter of an hour has passed. Must have been a dream. It felt real. It was real, I think. The unease from this daybreak rendezvous is enough to get me up. To be sure, I check the end of the bed, under the desk and behind the curtains – nothing.

Thirty minutes later my teeth are brushed, bowels evacuated, body washed and I'm back in my bedroom putting on my ill-fitting grey suit, off-white shirt and black tie. Leaping onto the bed, I retrieve my shoes from the far side. I recall being young, and leaping into bed in the same way. I was terrified that something would jump out from the darkness and grab me. I would normally say that I'm way too concerned with real life to worry about monsters nowadays, but something about that darkness has unnerved me today. Maybe it's the dream. I can remember it perfectly. More than that, I can feel it. Exhilaration seared into me. Why would I dream about a woman in Heaven? What does 'Don't rush to me, I'll wait,' mean? 'I guess you can still have hangover dreams without a hangover,' I comment to the still-silent hamster cage.

Even with my unusually chipper mood the thought of a day at work makes me nauseous. Maybe I could pull a sicky. No, did that last week... Wow... déjà vu.

XIV

46 minutes before

Leaving my strange morning behind, I nip out of the door and down the steps at the front of my house. I've got plenty of time to catch the 8.40 bus on Cowley Road. Damn, I need another shit. Have to put it out of my mind till I get to work.

It doesn't take me long to reach the church cut-through. My usual gravestones are waiting for me. *In Loving Memory of Madeline and Adam*; *Rest in Peace Captain Peters*; *Loving Mother and Father, Betty and Bob*, and finally, *Here lies Annie Waits*. The usual elderly man is tending Annie's grave.

'Morning,' I greet.

'Give me a hand, boy?' he shouts back with very little ceremony.

'Pardon,' I murmur, not quite catching the request.

'Give me a hand?' he grunts again.

I pause. 'Um sure,' I say. 'I've got time before the bus.'

'That's the spirit.' He grins. 'Won't take long.' He nods towards two large pieces of marble. 'I just need to put these on the grave.'

I slip my suit jacket off and fold it over a nearby gravestone.

The old man takes hold of a corner of the first stone. It's inscribed with the words *May she live on in*. It's heavier than it looks, but with a pretty unorthodox technique we edge it into place. 'I take it you knew her,' I say, dusting off my hands.

The aged skin round his eyes crumples as he looks down to the small headstone. 'I did. She was my first love,' he tells me as we heft the second stone. This one has *Heaven's embrace* on it.

'So it's you that Annie Waits for?' I say.

'I hope so,' he replies, with far more sincerity than I expected.

'May she live on in Heaven's embrace,' I read. 'Do you believe that?'

'I do, it's my faith.' He stoops down to tenderly touch the stone. 'Keeps her a presence in my life. What about you?'

'The Afterlife?' I ask.

He grunts an agreement.

'I'm actually starting to wonder,' I feel compelled to say, bearing in mind my strange morning.

'Well, it's a philosophy that kept me sane,' he says, reaching out one of his old hands. 'Thanks for stopping.' He takes my little fingers in his stride. I didn't expect anything else.

'No problem, happy to help,' I say, slipping my jacket on. He walks with me back to the path. 'I'm sorry you've been without her all this time,' I say to fill the silence.

'Don't be, I've had a wonderful life,' he says with a glint in his eye.

'Really?' I question.

'Why wouldn't I? I found and loved the one. Annie is there, waiting for me. But she'd want me to enjoy this life first. No pressure, no need to rush to her.' With that he pats me on the arm and turns back.

I stand stunned. 'Don't rush to me, I'll wait,' I say to myself. I glance at my watch – 8.36. 'Damn it, I'm going to miss the 8.40.'

Huge dark clouds roll over Oxford's jagged peaks, a contrast to the morning sun still warming my back. I leave the church's grand iron gates and hurriedly stride the last block to the bus stop. I skip down a long flight of concrete steps; sometimes I imagine throwing myself down them to get a day or two off work. Not today, though. I'm feeling good. And I never actually would do it; I hate pain too much.

The 8.40 is pulling up! Running the last few metres, I propel myself through the bus's closing doors. I climb to the top deck and drop into the first free seat. I watch large drops of rain hit the window.

A ticket inspector wobbles her way up the stairs. She looks tired as she shuffles down the aisle. Balls, what did I do with my ticket? Hastily, I start to rummage through my pockets. How have I got this many small pieces of paper? The inspector thanks the person ahead of me and turns in my direction. 'I've got it somewhere,' I say, checking my back pockets again. I've found a book of stamps, five receipts, two sweet wrappers and three old bus tickets, but I can't find the ticket I just fucking bought.

'What's your name?' she asks, readying herself to write up another fare-dodging chancer.

'Milton Pitt,' I answer, absently rifling through the many hidden areas of my wallet.

'Don't forget your top pocket, Mr Pitt.'

A twinge of familiarity jolts me from my search. Wordlessly, I place my hand on my breast pocket. There's something hard in there, about an inch long. I drop my little fingers into the pocket and fish out my ticket, and a small bottle with a label tied with string. 'Here you go.' I half-smile and hand her the ticket.

'Thanks,' she murmurs, giving the bottle a suspicious look as she moves on to the next passenger. I don't blame her – it is odd. How the hell did this get in my pocket? It's made of green glass and is oval like a sea-smoothed pebble on a beach. The bottle is sealed by a little cork and filled with some sort of thick, pure white substance. Not a liquid, it moves in a circular motion. The label says – *inhale me*. What the fuck? Only one way to find out, I guess. Twisting the cork free, I give it a gentle sniff. At a far greater velocity than I expect, the entire contents break free of the bottle and sling-shot into my nostrils. My head lurches back as the thick smoke seizes my senses, reverberates through my jaw and burrows deep into my temples. 'Fuck!' I cry as my breath is sucked back into my lungs. Like the detonation of an underwater minefield, multitudes of new memories explode into life. Dulled images ignite into technicolour and parade sounds, smells, tastes of new situations through my senses. My skull creaks and strains to contain the pathways being woven by the smoke. My jaw flexes as my mind divides, splitting between reality and something... something else... a new reality? New voices, new faces, strange places rapidly take shape, morphing from thought to fact. Visions take form: dying, flying, meeting Annie, *meeting God,* Heaven, that crazy little bastard's teeth severing my knuckles, my bald woman, then black. Worlds collide, the tide recedes, my head rocks back into a new reality.

I open my eyes to a mildly concerned collection of fellow commuters. 'Are you okay, dear?' The ticket inspector catches me off guard on her way back down the gangway.

'Yes,' I wheeze. 'Just a bit of a headache,' I say, stretching the skin round my throbbing eyes. This seems to appease her and the rest of the bus as they go about their business.

I lean my head on the cool glass of the window – it helps me relax. It feels like my brain has just been force-fed a big fucking Gothic banquet, and now it needs to lie back and digest. I died! I actually died.

I tentatively prod the freshly tattooed memories. This new information is so clear, but there's something strange about it. Oh shit! This isn't my view of what happened, it's my Narration's view. He's been narrating on me this whole time! All my new memories are either from the viewpoint of my Narration's little desk hideaway, or when he was standing directly in front of me.

My head throbs. I'm travelling to my death, for the second time! How am I meant to react to that? I should be glad to just be alive – shouldn't I? I'll do what I usually do when faced with a difficult situation. I take a breath, and just stop thinking. Switch off. Ignore it. Give the answer time to come to me.

For the rest of the journey I absently gaze out of the window. Every so often I glance to the mums, or their children, but they all seem to be on mute. The grimy alleyways of Cowley soon morph into the wide stone-blocked boulevards of Oxford's centre. I only notice my stop as the bus pulls up sharply and swings to the side of the road. The jolt brings me back to the present. Suddenly, everything makes sense. You can always trust thinking about nothing to give you the answers you need. I know what comes next!

Both mums gather their bags, coats and children.

I feel like I'm following a reminiscence as I trail them downstairs. They retrieve their buggies, drag them off the bus, and assemble them as effortlessly as they did the first time.

I don't have to check for my door pass to know that I've lost it. I look up at my office building – I hate the person that place makes me. In Purgatory my life was an adventure; I want that back. I take a lungful of crisp morning air to compose myself. 'Don't rush to me, I'll wait,' she said. 'But what if I don't want to wait?' Surveying the area, I find the little boy and girl already staring at the dead frog. I decide to play out the last act. 'I think you two should stand on the pavement, don't you?' I say. They look up. '*Eek*. Is that a dead frog?' I feel like I'm running lines as I scrutinise the squashed amphibian.

'Yes,' replies the girl on cue.

Again, the boy is quiet as he scrunches his T-shirt. Still not comfortable talking to strangers.

'Fog's eye's out,' the girl continues.

'So it is,' is my reply, 'so it is.' I sigh to myself. 'Maybe you two should go back to your mums.' I usher them to the pavement, but ignore the smiles of appreciation this time. Instead, I glance down the street. Sure enough, a blue hatchback is speeding towards me. I smile and step out.

XV

10 seconds after

My leg hangs in mid-air, body frozen. The car accelerates past and screeches round a tight corner. I step back onto the kerb. 'Perhaps I'll give this place a go first,' I say, glancing down to where I imagine my Narration now watches. 'Don't rush to me, I'll wait,' I meditate. 'I really shouldn't start by ignoring her advice, should I?' I grin to him. 'Plus, I really do hate pain.'

Walking a little more than five metres along the road, I look down to the place where I died. I still recall the misery of lying there in a crumpled heap, blood streaming from me. As I did, my eyes drift up until I'm gazing at the rooftops that I fluttered round as a butterfly.

'I'm still not happy with you, by the way.' I look back to him. 'Can't believe you bit my fingers off,' I say, gripping the stumps. 'That was savage. You've got issues mate, big fucking issues.' I eyeball the empty space for several seconds to make sure he knows I'm serious.

Turning from the scene, I begin to walk back in the direction of Cowley. I'm in no rush, not now. 'I guess

I'll have to forgive you at some point,' I sigh, 'and I do understand why you did it. I hope you're square with God now. I hope we both are. And thanks for the heads-up.' I pat the bottle, now back in my top pocket.

I pace up the gently sloping rise of old Magdalen Bridge. Punts are lined up along the riverside like the years of my life ahead of me, fading round the river's bend. I lean on the cool stone balustrade. 'Such a stupid way of travelling, isn't it? Hundreds of years of academia and they still push boats round with poles.' I imagine my Narration rolling his eyes as he types out such a pointless statement – it puts a smile on my face. 'It's weird knowing you're watching me,' I remark. 'Going to the toilet is gonna be a nightmare with you lot there. I'm not good in front of an audience. Probably worse for you, though.' I grin. 'I'm going to have to make a real effort to ignore you.' A passer-by gives me an odd look. It stops me in my tracks and stirs something, a memory. It's the look I gave my Narration the first time he started talking to his invisible friends. That's not a good sign – I should probably start ignoring him sooner rather than later.

I still see no reason to pop his delusion, but it's definitely time to cut all ties. 'Send my best to Kazuo, Lady Jane and Arik,' I say. 'Tell them I'll quit my job today, rent out my flat tomorrow, and book a flight... somewhere, the day after. That should give you lot something more interesting to watch.' I give my Narration a subtle salute. 'Let's see if I can't find you a little bit of Heaven on Earth.'

Acknowledgements

I'm eternally grateful to my parents, step-parents and grandparents for bringing me up with love, kindness and happiness. Even amid hardship and illness, you all made sacrifices to give me opportunities to broaden my horizons and discover the breadth and richness of the life that was available to me.

Thank you to my beautiful wife for your devoted love, faith in me, and for knowing me better than anyone else. To my daughter, for lighting up my life in ways I couldn't have imagined – may you read this when you're older and enjoy the strange things Daddy wrote down.

In addition, Mum, without your unceasing belief in me and my writing, this book would not have happened. Thank you for seeing the potential of this book even when it was just a dot in the distance, and for your unwavering patience as draft by draft you helped me discover it.

To my two best mates, Tim and Zeb, throughout my life you've been best men in all senses of the word.

Ever since I started composing stories I'd hoped to one day be published, but always quietly accepted that this may never happen. My deepest thanks to all at Fairlight for not only showing me my writing has value but putting it into print. To Louise, for taking a unique approach to the publishing industry and placing great writing, whoever writes it, at the heart of what you do. To Urška, for taking the time to understand and appreciate my story and adding a huge amount of value in the editing process. I look forward to working further with the entire Fairlight family.

Bookclub and writers' circle notes for the
Fairlight Moderns can be found at
www.fairlightmoderns.com

Share your thoughts about the book
with **#MiltoninPurgatory**

Also in the Fairlight Moderns series

SOPHIE VAN LLEWYN

Bottled Goods

*Longlisted for The Women's Prize for Fiction 2019,
People's Book Prize for Fiction 2018 and The Republic
of Consciousness Prize 2019*

When Alina's brother-in-law defects to the West,
she and her husband become persons of interest to
the secret services and both of their careers come
grinding to a halt.

As the strain takes its toll on their marriage,
Alina turns to her aunt for help – the wife of a
communist leader and a secret practitioner of the
old folk ways.

Set in 1970s communist Romania, this novella-
in-flash draws upon magic realism to weave a
captivating tale of everyday troubles.

*'It is a story to savour, to smile at, to
rage against and to weep over.'*
—Zoe Gilbert, author of *FOLK*

*'Sophie van Llewyn has brought light
into an era which cast a long shadow.'*
—Joanna Campbell, author of
Tying Down the Lion

ANTHONY FERNER

Inside the Bone Box

*'On a good day at work, the tips of his fingers seemed
to tingle with focused energy. They sensed the space,
rose, turned through angles, intuited the tissue, felt the
consistency of flesh, used just the right degree of delicacy
or brutality.'*

Nicholas Anderton is a highly respected
neurosurgeon at the top of his field. But behind
the successful façade all is not well. Tormented by
a toxic marriage and haunted by past mistakes,
Anderton has been eating to forget. His wife,
meanwhile, has turned to drink.

There are sniggers behind closed doors – how can
a surgeon be fat? When mistakes are made and his
old adversary steps in to take advantage, Anderton
knows things are coming to a head...

*'A little book that packs a punch far greater
than its size.'* —The Idle Woman, blogger